alyssa brugman

walking

naked

158
34

Published by
Laurel-Leaf
an imprint of
Random House Children's Books
a division of Random House, Inc.
New York

Visit us on the Web! www.randomhouse.com/teens

Educators and librarians, for a variety of teaching tools, visit us at www.randomhouse.com/teachers

ISBN: 0-440-23832-3

Reprinted by arrangement with Delacorte Press

Printed in the United States of America

September 2005

10 9 8 7 6 5 4 3 2 1

OPM

For my beautiful sister Corrina, who thought it sounded like an awful story

Many thanks to one of my favorite people, Claire, who kindly allowed me to rant at her while I was writing this book

Tyger! Tyger! burning bright
In the forests of the night,
What immortal hand or eye
Could frame thy fearful symmetry?

In what distant deeps or skies
Burnt the fire of thine eyes?
On what wings dare he aspire?
What the hand dare seize the fire?

And what shoulder, & what art,
Could twist the sinews of thy heart?
And when thy heart began to beat,
What dread hand? & what dread feet?

What the hammer? What the chain?
In what furnace was thy brain?
What the anvil? What dread grasp
Dare its deadly terrors clasp?

When the stars threw down their spears,
And water'd heaven with their tears,
Did He smile His work to see?
Did He who made the lamb make thee?

Tyger! Tyger! burning bright
In the forests of the night,
What immortal hand or eye,
Dare frame thy fearful symmetry?

William Blake

1

I am responsible for a great many things, but being put on detention for talking in history was not my fault (not technically, anyway).

On that Monday, I was not nearly so interested in history as in Candice Perkins's story about what happened at Michael Sorrell's party on Saturday night.

Parties and dating were not usually my thing—that was Candice's domain—but there had been an arrest, and that piqued my interest.

Candice and Michael had been going out for about three months. They talked on the phone a couple of times a week and kissed at school socials, but that was about it.

The exciting thing that happened at Michael Sorrell's party (which was, technically, Michael's older brother's party) was that the police caught two of the Year 12 boys doing a nudey run.

"There were about six of them but only two of them got busted," explained Candice. "The others ran down the lane and hid behind the scout hall. One of them, Jacob—do you know Jacob?—he's over eighteen and might go to court. Can you believe it?"

I thought Candice seemed pleased with herself—it was quite a coup to be invited to a party with the Year 12s.

Candice and I had been best friends since kindergarten. We had all sorts of stupid sayings that had become ritual between us. We always said "Like, oh, yar, I know, totally," in a Valley girl voice.

Candice and I were the founders of "the group." I was the brains, she was the beauty, and in Year 4 we had begun to hang out with Jessica Chou as well. Jessica was pretty and smart, but not enough of either for Candice or me to feel threatened. It wasn't until Year 6 that we started recruiting in earnest, but I'll get to that.

On this particular day, our history teacher, Ms. Sloan, had asked us to be quiet more than once (I strongly suspected that Ms. Sloan was hypoglycemic, because lessons after lunch went much more smoothly than lessons before) and so we were, technically, being quiet. Of course, what Ms. Sloan meant was "be silent"—and if she had been clear on that point, then I might not have ended up in detention.

Candice and I were whispering quietly when Ms. Sloan said, "Right! That's it! Out!"

I'd never been sent out in my life. Candice had—mostly for talking. I politely slid in my chair so that Candice could leave.

Ms. Sloan found this gesture somewhat provocative. "Both of you!"

"What, *me*?"

"Yes, *you*!"

I wasn't familiar with thrown-out-of-class protocol. "Do I take my bag? Or will it just be for a short time? Where do we go? Do we just stand outside the door? Or is it sort of like an early mark?"

I wasn't being difficult, I swear. I was just trying to establish the procedure.

"Out! Out! Out!"

A moment later Candice and I were out in the hall.

"So you reckon Jacob is going to court?" I asked.

"I know, can you believe it? Michael said that all of the Year Twelve boys that are seventeen are going to hold a Grand Nudey Run in protest. When they get busted they can't get a record. I mean, it's just ridiculous."

"Ridiculous," I agreed. It didn't occur to me at the time that Candice and I might not have meant the same thing.

A movement at the end of the hallway caught my

attention. I turned my head and saw Perdita Wiguiggan crossing the hallway. She was scooting along with her head down and a stack of books pressed against her chest.

I made the sign of the cross. Candice did the same and said, "Freak," loudly enough for Perdita to hear, but not loudly enough to draw attention to us.

Every school has one. They are ugly or fat. They have scars or acne or birthmarks. Or maybe it's just something about them that doesn't quite fit with our cherry-lipgloss, video-hits view of how teenagers should be?

We are mean to them. We call them names. We ridicule them. We make monsters of them. We don't want to stand near them or sit next to them. They repulse us.

Perdita Wiguiggan was one of those. How unfortunate for her to have a name that was hard to say—*Purdeetah Wigweegan*—on top of being the most despised creature in the whole school.

If you had asked me how I felt about her I would have said that I hated her, but I couldn't have told you why. "I just hate her," I would have said with a dismissive shrug.

Maybe it was the way she walked. Perdita Wiguiggan hunkered down with her shoulders stooped and her chin forward. She took long clomping strides like a man. It was a very ungraceful walk.

Three things can happen to people like Perdita Wiguiggan. One, they become incredibly successful. They

4

are your rocket scientists, your academics. Einstein was one of them. They found billion-dollar dot-com companies. They become rock stars—Kurt Cobain was probably one. Janis Joplin certainly was.

Two, they can stay shunned and pitied and live shallow lives on the periphery of society. They get low-paid jobs and roll from one dysfunctional, abusive relationship to another because they don't believe that they deserve to be treated any better. Why should they? No one ever *has*.

Or they can end up like Perdita, but I'll get to that.

After Perdita had gone, Mr. Tilly, who was our deputy principal and one of my very favorites, walked past and said, "Megan Tuw, what are *you* doing out here?"

My name is Megan Tuw. I suppose it's quite convenient, as there are frequent occasions at which I am not the only Megan. It does mean, though, that I am never the primary Megan. I am, at best, only the runner-up Megan.

This was the case when Megan Hadenham was recruited into the group. I was opposed to Megan Hadenham from the beginning. She didn't seem to have anything new to bring to the group, and besides, having more than one Megan would be confusing. Jessica Chou pointed out that we couldn't exactly ask her to change her name.

"Maybe we could call you Tuwy?" suggested Dara Drinkwater. I didn't like Dara Drinkwater. She was always casually suggesting that I compromise. I don't like to compromise. Dara's offhand recommendations always got up my nose.

"Do you know where the name Peterson came from, Dara?" I asked. "And the names Davidson, Williamson, Harrison or Jameson?"

"What are you talking about?"

"They all mean 'son of': son of Peter, son of David, son of William, and so on. Do you get it? Peter and David and William came first. If you did it the other way around you would have all of these people wandering about called Peterdad, Daviddad, Williamdad. See?"

Dara tossed her head. "You're not Megan Hadenham's dad, *Tuwy*."

"The person who comes first gets the name, *Drinky*."

"Maybe we could allocate her a nickname, like Haddy or something?" suggested Jessica Chou. Jessica was always stepping in to defuse fights between Dara and me.

Unfortunately this never transpired. From that day onward Megan Hadenham was Megan, and I became Megan Tuw. This is a matter that I still consider to be *grossly* unfair.

Meanwhile, back in the hallway. "I've been sent out," I replied indignantly to Mr. Tilly.

"Really? What did you do?" he asked with a twinkle in his eye. Mr. Tilly was genuinely amused by the company of youths. That was why he was one of my very favorites.

"I was talking."

Just as I was about to bring Mr. Tilly up to speed on

the whole quiet versus silence discrepancy, Ms. Sloan decided that our exile was over. She opened the door, and because I was leaning against it, I fell backward into the room and landed on my bum.

Mr. Tilly and Candice thought this was tremendously funny. Ms. Sloan did not.

"Quite the clown, aren't we?"

"Well, Ms. Sloan, technically, I am the only clown in this scenario," I said, standing and straightening my school skirt with as much dignity as I could muster, having just sprawled across the floor. "So perhaps the use of the plural is not entirely appropriate."

Ms. Sloan's eyes narrowed into uncharitable slits. "A week's detention, miss."

That's how I ended up in detention. As you can see, technically, I was entirely blameless.

I made my song a coat
Covered with embroideries
Out of old mythologies
From heel to throat;
But the fools caught it,
Wore it in the world's eyes
As though they'd wrought it.
Song, let them take it,
For there's more enterprise
In walking naked.

W. B. Yeats

I knew who Perdita was, though we had never exchanged words. Looking at her objectively, I would have to say she was neither short nor tall, thin nor overweight, ugly nor pretty. She had wild, thick, dark hair. If she wore it down it would have hung to her waist, but she never did. It was all piled up untidily at the top of her head and stuck there with pins.

At the time, though, hearsay had made her so grotesque to me that I avoided looking at her altogether.

According to reports I had heard, she talked to herself. She said weird things, sometimes in Old English. I heard that once she stood on her desk and chanted in Latin. She wouldn't sit down and had to be physically removed from the room.

I heard that she was part of a cult, that she was a witch. One time in primary school, apparently, she had called someone a spotted something (nobody could remember exactly what), and within a month a wave of chicken pox had hit the school.

I heard that she smelt. I heard that she didn't wash or brush her hair and that once someone had seen a tiny cockroach scuttle down behind her left ear and then disappear again in the hair at the nape of her neck.

When I walked into the detention room and saw her there, I quickly lowered my eyes and moved to the other end of the room.

Perdita sat in the corner furthest from the door with her face in a book. As I sat down she looked up and leered at me, exposing some of her crooked teeth. I am a big believer in oral hygiene. I think that, in this day and age, with the technology and pharmaceuticals available, people should be more attentive to this matter than they generally are. There is no excuse for it.

"By the pricking of my thumbs," she said.

I ignored her. I turned away and played with my hair.

"Did He smile His work to see? Did He who made the lamb make thee?" she said. Weirdo.

Again I ignored her, and after a moment she buried herself back in the book.

I just thought she was a nutcase. I didn't know what she was talking about. I do now. The first thing she said is a quote from *Macbeth*. It is spoken by one of the witches. I've since heard it in the drama room at the Sydney Opera House. When the actor said it I felt a prickle of recognition. The next line is "something wicked this way comes." When the actor said *that,* I wanted to laugh and cry at the same time. Why? We'll get to that.

The second quote is from a well-known poem by William Blake called "The Tyger." Back then I would have said it's about the inherent unfairness of nature, but then, I don't believe in God. Nowadays I have a little more compassion for lambs.

Either way, Perdita knew who I was, and she thought I was bad. Of course, I didn't have the slightest interest in what Perdita thought of me. Grrrr.

On this first afternoon of detention, Perdita and I were the only ones in the classroom.

We were being supervised by a nondescript industrial arts teacher who was referred to by the unimaginative nickname Browney (his surname was Brown).

Browney wore exactly the same stonewashed denim outfit every day. Which to me was inexplicable, considering that he was allowed to wear whatever he wanted. I could only assume that, somewhere in the mid-1980s, he'd found an outfit that worked for him and purchased an enormous quantity that would last him the rest of his life.

When I entered, Browney had written an exercise for us on the chalkboard and then sat down at the desk at the front of the room to mark papers.

This was the exercise:

Given your recent behavior, please justify (in approximately 300 words) why you should be allowed to be a full participant in the school community.

I wrote:

I believe that I am a valuable contributor to the school community. The particulars of my contribution, which I will list below, and my general behavior to date justify my participation in the school community.

I am among the top ten in all my classes. I am a representative on the regional netball and swimming teams. I was an active member in the school band until my studies required more of my attention. I am also on the school social organizing committee.

Because of my being at the school, my mother is a volunteer in the canteen, and both my parents regularly attend the Parents & Citizens' Association, therefore, my being here also brings a contribution to the school from the general public.

The reason for my being on detention is that I was talking in class, and therefore, allegedly, disrupting the learning of others. I would respectfully argue that the only student whose learning I was disrupting was Candice Perkins. The word "disrupt" suggests some force and, given that Candice was a willing participant in the discussion, technically my behavior was not "disruptive" at all.

With this in mind, and with the highest of regard to Ms. Sloan, I would point out that the act of removing us from the classroom and then allowing us to return was more disruptive to the class, as a whole, than the actions that caused us to be removed in the first place.

Furthermore, I consider myself lucky not to have suffered any permanent damage to my coccyx during the incident. I certainly hope that the school has kept up to date with its public liability insurance.

In conclusion, I am, in general, a valuable contributor to the school community. The "recent behavior" for which I have been detained is not typical of me (and technically, was not disruptive, anyway).

I humbly put forward that perhaps my behavior to date should have been taken into consideration before this punishment was enforced.

In the time it took me to write this, Perdita wrote two responses.

This is the one she handed in:

> Icky, bicky, snicky, spay,
> Doesn't matter what I say,
> Staffed with Ratcheds anyway.

Browney read it aloud and then placed it on the desk in front of him. He folded his arms and asked Perdita to explain herself. She chose not to.

"Can I assume, then, that the 'Ratched' you refer to is Nurse Ratched from *One Flew over the Cuckoo's Nest?*"

Perdita nodded.

"Did you not think that I might find the comparison insulting?"

"I assumed, if you understood it at all, that you would," she replied. She was smiling smugly. I put my hand to my forehead. Why couldn't she just be *normal?* It would save everyone so much time.

"Then you're not very wise," said Browney. "We cannot have students, even the very bright ones, behaving in an unruly, insolent and undisciplined manner. It would be chaos. You know the rules and you have the capacity to uphold them. The fact that you choose not to is pure obstinacy. You know this."

"You mean, why can't I use my powers for good instead of evil?"

"If you like."

Perdita said nothing. She just stood there, smiling her smug smile.

Browney sighed. "Another week of detention, Perdita." Then he went back to his marking. A couple of minutes later he gathered his papers in a pile and dismissed us.

As we were leaving, there was an awkward moment. I stood up, throwing my bag over my shoulder. Perdita rushed toward me. I could see her approaching from the corner of my eye. (I have acute peripheral vision. It gives me an advantage in team sports and catfights.)

I hurried toward the door, bumping my thigh on the edge of the desk. I didn't want to be in the same space as Perdita. I felt a need to get as far away from her as I could. I didn't want to breathe the same air, or smell her. As she approached, I held my breath.

We both reached the door at the same time. Perdita thrust a piece of paper toward me. I took it almost by instinct, but I avoided her eyes. Then we both headed down the corridor, in opposite directions.

I crumpled up the paper, shoved it in my pocket and forgot about it. If there had been a trash bin nearby I would have thrown the paper in without looking at it.

Later that night I was sitting at the dining room table pretending to do my homework while I was watching television. My mother came out of the laundry room, where she had been washing and ironing my school clothes.

"Did you write this?" she said to me with a twinkle in

her eye. She was holding Perdita's paper. It took me a moment to recognize it.

"Oh, no, it was just this girl."

"It's great, isn't it? Such a fabulous grasp of irony," she said as she smoothed it out with her hand. "Go and show it to Dad."

"No, Mum, I'm doing my homework."

"It'll only take a minute."

My mother was always showing things to my father. Every day when he came home from work they would have a little show-and-tell session. I always thought she must have spent her whole day saving up little things to show him or tell him about. They would open a bottle of wine and sit out on the deck, or in the living room if it was winter, just talking.

They kissed all the time too. It was disgusting. They even kissed in front of my friends. They had absolutely no shame.

They spoke to me as one unit—"We think this" or "We think that." Neither of them was an individual; they were an exclusive club of two.

My mother was such a good little woman. It got up my nose. Why couldn't they be their own people?

I took the paper, sighing and thumping to indicate to my mother just how inconvenient it was, to my father, who was sitting in his chair in the living room.

My father had always retired to his chair after dinner, ever since I could remember. It was also the seat from which he read my school reports. At the end of every school year he would sit in his chair, put on his glasses and read excerpts to my mother.

" 'Megan has a natural aptitude for this subject.' Did you read this, Eileen? A natural—that's my girl."

My parents were so predictable. I had a fantasy about waiting until they were out one day and then moving all the furniture in the house one meter to the left—Mr. and Mrs. Tuw's own personal Twilight Zone.

My father wasn't wearing his glasses, so he asked me to read the essay aloud. I did.

This is what Perdita had written:

A school is a place of hopes—a coral of potential. The school community is the spirit, the sculptor's chisel wielded by the staff that chips at the unformed intellect, releases each student from the shackles of ignorance, and gives them form. It is a spirit that is shared—one vision, one motto, one song.

The success of our school against others arises from this inherent strength. Unformed and ignorant, we earn the school spirit, and in our turn the school spirit earns us—a new cohort, *Citius, Altius, Fortius,* faster, higher, stronger.

It is the school community spirit that makes this transformation possible. It gives each student a standard to uphold. We understand the expectation, and with the aid of the constant chips of the chisel we can strive to meet this one ideal.

This is why it is entirely appropriate that miscreants like myself, those who cannot, or will not, sing the song, those flawed by thoughts conflicting with the spirit of the school, should not be allowed to participate in the school community.

Ad nocendum potentes sumus! We have the power to harm.

We are the tarnish on the honor board, the indolent medicine ball, the faded blazer.

Society will know students from this school by the colors we wear. They will hear one song, sung together with fervor as we march out the gates and amongst them.

Similarly, miscreants like myself should be marked in some way, so that others can identify us and not be poisoned by us, or mistake us for the true graduates of the one vision.

I propose that until such time as we can be isolated, or removed entirely from the school community, we be marked with a symbol (perhaps a star?), and in this way our wickedness will be known to all.

After I had finished, my father raised his eyebrows. "A miscreant—is that irony, do you think? Or perhaps a cleverly crafted cry for help?"

I shrugged. I didn't really care.

3

The group had netball training every Monday night. We played indoor netball as training for the competition games on Saturday. I loved netball. I loved pounding up and down the court. I loved working really hard till my muscles felt rubbery. I loved it because I was good at it.

We laughed a lot too, in the training games. But we only laughed on Monday nights. The Saturday games were business.

Candice and I had been playing on the same team for eight seasons. Candice was better than I was. She was center and I was wing attack.

Candice always thought two moves ahead. I really enjoyed watching her play. She would quickly scan the court, her eyes fierce with concentration, and then she would pass, not waiting to see if the ball was caught before moving into the next position.

She saw holes in defense where there were no holes. She seemed to know where people *weren't* going to be even before they did.

In the training games Candice would do flying leaps in the air. She would start running and shout, "Throw it, throw it!" and then whoever had the ball would pass it to her. She would leap into the air and catch it, land on one foot and throw it wildly over her shoulder before she skidded off the court. The rest of us had to scramble to wherever the ball was going to land.

Most of the time, two or even three of us would run to the spot. We would all be watching the ball, not each other, and we would all end up on the floor in a giggling, tangled heap of arms and legs. The rest of us sustained a lot of bruises and grazes from Candice's flying leaps, but we were sure that one day her maneuver would come in handy.

The group made a good team. We had been playing together with an unchanged lineup for three seasons and we had never forfeited a game. Just from a glance we would each know where each player was. We played fast and strategically, that was our advantage.

Dara Drinkwater was very good—but not as good as she thought she was. Dara was a bit of a ball hog. She used other players, usually Jessica, to reposition herself on the court all the time. They would do this backward-and-forward passing thing until Dara was where she wanted to be. Sometimes it just would have been easier to give someone else the ball. It got right up my nose.

They did have some good moves, though, like the tricky backward-dummy pass. Dara would catch the ball and do a little pirouette. Jessica would then move in behind her. Dara would dummy the pass to someone else and pop it over her shoulder to Jessica. The opponents would look at Dara, and Jessica would throw it back over Dara's head to whomever she had dummied to on the other side. It worked a treat.

Ashley Anderson was our shooter. She missed half the goals, but our team always had twice as many shots at goal anyway. Ashley liked being goal shooter and we let her because her mum did so much for the team and her sister, Crystal, played whenever we were short. Ashley's mum made our uniforms and they were the best. Some teams had really ugly uniforms, but we had matching outfits in white and powder blue. We all had shirts with our names embroidered on the back of them.

On this particular Monday night, Crystal wasn't playing. Katie Gattrell was. Katie Gattrell was a new recruit.

She had been recruited under the normal procedure. Jessica Chou was our unofficial talent scout.

Jessica's parents were both doctors. Her mother was

a whizbang specialist in gastroenterology or neurology or podiatry or something. Jessica's mum was always flying around the world to give lectures. Jessica's father was a GP. I think they had an expectation that Jessica would do medicine, but I had a strong suspicion that she would end up in human resources.

Jessica's parents also suffered from an acute humor deficiency, so I was fairly certain that it would all end in tears.

When Jessica selected Katie Gattrell, the group sat in a circle and listened to Jessica's assessment. Everyone was attentive except for Dara Drinkwater, who was leaning back with one leg crossed carelessly over the other and filing her nails. Dara Drinkwater was always flinging herself about carelessly. She always looked so casually impeccable. It really got up my nose.

Jessica's assessment of Katie Gattrell was as follows: she was bright and cheerful, she had a nice figure and a discerning eye for fashion, and she seemed to have a reasonably good relationship with teachers. That was important. The group didn't want troublemakers; we couldn't afford to have our grades suffer by association.

"Does she play sport?" asked Candice.

"Soccer," replied Jessica.

"Mixed?" asked Ashley.

"I think so," replied Jessica.

"That sounds like fun," said Ashley.

"Yes, but who has she gone out with?" asked Dara, looking up from her nails for a moment.

Dara Drinkwater was just not my sort of person. Candice picked her for the group. I had no idea why. I thought Candice's judgment was poor.

Dara had short, shiny auburn hair and long, meticulously manicured nails, which she was constantly preening. I was sure she would end up being one of those thin, irritatingly well-groomed women.

After slumber parties everyone else looked puffy and drained—Dara only ever looked *tousled*. I found it really annoying.

Megan Hadenham was my second-least favorite. I had never forgiven her for the whole name-stealing business.

Ashley Anderson had never had an original thought in her whole life. I found her altogether inoffensive and nonthreatening.

"Hmmm," said Jessica, riffling through her notes, "she's gone out with Paul Welwood, Chris Baxter, Lindon McNitt."

"Has she gone out with anyone in Michael's group?" asked Candice.

"I think Paul Welwood was in Michael's group in Year Eight," said Ashley.

"That was ages ago. Find out if she likes someone," said Candice.

Due to a strong academic record and a prior liaison with Paul Welwood, Katie Gattrell earned herself a trial membership.

Katie Gattrell was hopeless at netball. Every time the

ball came near her she would watch it with eyes that were forty percent desperate and sixty percent terrified. When she actually caught it, she seemed surprised and relieved. She would grin and throw it to someone else.

Katie Gattrell was hopeless at passing, too. You're supposed to turn the ball around so the backs of your hands are facing your chest and then push out. Katie Gattrell threw the ball underarm. She might have been good at soccer, but as far as netball was concerned she was an absolute shocker.

Katie really liked those Monday-night games, though. I don't know how someone so useless could have so much fun. There was no way I was going to let her within two kilometers of a Saturday game, but the training games didn't matter. She loved it. She would shriek and grin and laugh. Katie made such a spectacle of herself that I could hardly bear to watch.

There was a cafeteria on the ground floor of the indoor sports center. After the games we would sit downstairs. Michael Sorrell had an indoor cricket team and so we would sit outside their court, having a cool drink and watching them play.

Katie stood there with a silly grin on her face. Her cheeks were all flushed from the exercise. She shouted her support for the cricketers: "Good shot, Mathew," "Onya, Joshua." It was so gawky.

I didn't like Katie Gattrell but, as it turned out, I should have paid her closer attention.

4

Browney was writing on the chalkboard when I arrived for the next detention. He smiled a cold, brief smile as I entered the room. Perdita was sitting in the corner looking out the window.

"I have tailored your exercise for today around Ms. Wiguiggan's penchant for old movies." He put the chalk down and rubbed his hands together. He seemed to be quite pleased with himself. Sadist.

The exercise was as follows:

Name three characters in classic movies who have been too clever for their own good. Explain how their arrogance led to their downfall.

I took out my notepad, tapped my pen on my teeth for a minute and began.

In the movie *Titanic* the passengers on the boat were arrogant. It was an expensive ship, and so, to even board in the first place, they must have felt some sense of superiority over others. In the end they all died because of their vanity (except the character played by Kate Winslet, who learned about love and survived).

In *A Few Good Men* the Jack Nicholson character ends up going to jail because of his arrogance. He wants to tell the world how important he is because he thinks his contribution to the safety of the country is undervalued. It is this arrogance that makes him think he can break the law, and that people should even be grateful to him for his crime.

However, the Tom Cruise character made him say the words that put him in jail by using arrogance against him. The pivotal point in the movie was the battle between the two arrogant characters. The difference is that the Tom Cruise character, although arrogant, had virtue and honesty.

That's three, but I would like to point out that in any action movie that you care to name, the heroes are usually arrogant. They disobey authority. They follow their own gut instincts without listening to anyone else's expert advice (and quite often in opposition to it). They fight the bad guy alone. Arrogance might not make them popular, but it does have a tendency to save the world.

Browney collected both of our papers, read them quickly and gave them back to us.

When he dismissed us, I turned around in my chair to Perdita and cleared my throat. I had never spoken to her, although I had spoken *at* her many times. Everybody did. She was the Freak.

I was sure she didn't take it personally when we called her the Freak. That was just who she was. It was just something that we did, a bit like "Would you like fries with that?"—after a while it was automatic and you didn't even notice.

"Can I read yours?" I asked. I smiled at her to let her know that it was OK and that she could speak to me. It was a distant smile, though. She could speak to me *on this occasion*. She didn't smile back. She stood up, dropped her paper on my desk and left. It was very rude, considering who I *was*.

I sat at my desk for a while, reading.

Perdita's response was as follows:

What is arrogance? A combination of presumption, pride and assertiveness.

Orson Welles produced *Citizen Kane*—a movie with arrogance as a major theme. Kane manipulates the world around him for his own ends, and yet he remains discontented.

The act of producing the movie in itself was an act of arrogance on the part of Welles, for only a combination of presumption, pride and assertiveness could give rise to one so ruthlessly and shamelessly parodying the life of the rich and powerful–and more arrogant still, pitying them.

On the other hand, *Citizen Kane* is still considered to be one of the greatest movies ever produced. Welles' career was short. But one could question whether this was the result of arrogance or an unwillingness to compromise artistic integrity.

James Bond, in all his guises, is arrogant. We are fed the same story over and over again, and yet each one is a blockbuster. It is his presumption, pride and assertiveness that make him so admired by men and so attractive to women.

(The statement is a sweeping one. There are, of course, both men and women who are not impressed by Mr. Bond. There are also people who can't see past the zippers of the Ewoks, or the scientific impossibility of the transporter on the Starship *Enterprise*. It's a MOVIE, people!)

However, of all the obnoxiously arrogant characters ever fashioned for viewing, Snow White is the monarch. In the film *Snow White and the Seven Dwarfs*, Ms. White intrudes on the lives of seven independent young men, imposing on them her own style of home décor and standards of hygiene.

Ms. White then suffers a prolonged coma for being one of those supercilious, snooty health freaks who presume that apples are good for one, despite biblical evidence to the contrary (and one doesn't even have to read very far into said text to find reference to it–proving her to be not only arrogant but ungodly).

And so it is, ultimately, well deserved that she meets her fate–being abducted by an inbred aristocrat and forced to live with him ever after.

I folded it carefully and put it in my blazer pocket. When I got home I handed it to my mother.

She wasn't wearing her contacts so she held it at arm's length with her mouth downturned.

My mother is a botanist. She has been at university forever and has about a hundred degrees. She specializes in succulents. She has a deep passion for *pachyphytum oviferum,* or moonstones.

Every two years she completely overhauls our garden. She couldn't bear the idea of her plants dying and so for her fortieth birthday my father bought her fifteen acres on the Central Coast. He had a big wooden sign made for the front gate that said *Novitas Sepulchrum Arbustus,* which means something like "strange grave planted with trees." We called it Novitas for short. Every two years my mother transplants the entire garden to Novitas. It's a bit of a ritual.

My mother plants succulents to the exclusion of almost everything else. She can make a small suburban garden look like a groovy Mexican vista, but I can tell you, acre upon acre of closely packed succulents in the middle of the lush green Central Coast looks very strange indeed.

"Who is this girl?" my mother asked when she had finished.

"Her name is Perdita."

"Perdita what?"

"Perdita Wiguiggan."

My mother raised her eyebrows. "That's a silly name."

"You should talk about silly names," I said.

"What do you mean?" she said sharply.

"Like our last name is so sensible."

"Tuw is a fabulous name. It's your father's name, and he's a fabulous man. You should be proud."

My father's name is Hugh. Hugh Tuw and Eileen Tuw—you can't get much sillier than that—except perhaps Vanua, or Juan.

"OK, OK," I said, waving my arm at her before she continued with her pro-Dad speech.

"I want to meet this friend of yours with a silly name. Why don't you invite her over for dinner one night?" she asked.

I snorted.

"What?"

"She's not my *friend.* She's just on detention."

"Why isn't she your friend? She sounds like fun."

"She's not the sort of person that you be friends with."

"Why not?"

I rolled my eyes. "You wouldn't understand."

"Try me."

"She's weird. She's a Froot Loop. She doesn't do ordinary stuff. Everybody hates her. She cuts school half the time, so I don't know why you're so big on me being friends with her, anyway. I met her on *detention*, Mum, she's bad."

"You're on detention."

"Yes, but I'm on detention by *mistake*."

"You're on detention for being disagreeable. I know, because I read the letter. Now," she said, putting Perdita's paper on the bench and poking at it with her finger, "I want to meet Perdita Wiguiggan. I won't let this go, so you may as well do as you're told."

I exhaled loudly. I couldn't believe how unreasonable she was being. Bring the Freak home? What on earth was she thinking? My mother had no idea. It was absolutely out of the question.

Katie Gattrell was standing on shaky ground as far as I was concerned, and she knew it. I could tell because she had lost all sense of personal space. She kept patting our arms and standing too close. She laughed too loudly. She fawned and flattered beyond all proportion. Katie Gattrell was getting desperate.

The trial was almost over and Katie's performance had been less than adequate. She wasn't particularly good at sport. Her schoolwork was satisfactory, nothing special. But neither of these things really mattered to me. There was something much more insidious about her.

Katie Gattrell was a parasite. Take for instance Thursday-night shopping with the group. Katie Gattrell tried things on, but she never bought anything. It would then transpire, when we got to the food hall, that she had no money. Why try things on if you've got no money?

So the rest of us would buy our food and Katie would get a fork and help herself to each of our plates.

This I didn't mind so much. It was just a tangible display of the real problem. What really annoyed me was that Katie would then sit there and laugh at all the jokes, lean forward to hear all the gossip, but never contribute to either. She took but she never gave anything back. It really got up my nose.

Bitching and joke telling are both risky. Bitchiness can make you seem mean, or worse—the content of the bitchiness could get back to the person. Jokes can fall flat and make you look dumb. Katie Gattrell avoided those risks.

I talked to Candice about it. She was lying on her stomach on my living room floor, resting her cheek on her folded hands. Mum and Dad had gone out for dinner.

I liked the way Candice walked around my house as though it were her own. She helped herself to food from the fridge. She knew where everything was. I didn't have any brothers or sisters. Candice was almost like having a sister, maybe a stepsister—one that wasn't there all the time.

"What do you reckon about Katie?" I asked her.

"She's OK," Candice replied.

"Yeah, she's really nice, considering." I said that last word and then let it just hang there in the air. Candice would bite. I knew she would.

"Considering what?"

"Haven't you noticed that she's never got any money? I mean, we haven't got heaps, but we can always pay our own way. And she never joins in when we're talking."

"She doesn't say much about anything, really," said Candice.

"It must be a bit of a shock for her to hear us. You know, how we go on. I hope she doesn't get the wrong impression."

"What do you mean?"

"Well, we make jokes about people all the time, and of course we don't intend any harm, but because she's not that kind of person she might think we really mean what we say."

Candice frowned. I continued. "Like the other day when you were talking about that fat girl, Angela. Do you remember? And I was thinking about how Katie and Angela were friends for a while there and maybe she thought you were being mean. You weren't, but she might have thought you were and she might tell Angela what you said."

"I wasn't being mean," said Candice, sitting up.

"Of course not."

Candice lay back down again, looking thoughtful. "You don't reckon she'd really tell Angela what I said, do you?"

I shrugged. "I don't know her that well. Like you said,

she doesn't say much. But on the other hand, she's only on trial with us. She might feel she's closer to Angela."

A few days later Candice rang me to see if I wanted to go shopping. We had this dumb ritual when we rang each other up.

"May I speak to the lady of the house?" Candice would say in her posh voice.

"The lady of the house is speaking," I'd reply.

"To whom is she speaking?" said Candice.

Then we always laughed. I don't know why. Every day we said the same stupid joke.

"Do you reckon we should ask Katie to come tonight?"

"Why not?"

"Well, I've been talking with the others. Jessica wonders if it might make Katie feel bad that she's never got any money. And the others have been saying that they just don't feel they can talk openly in front of her anymore."

"But, Candice, we can't just ignore her. That wouldn't be fair. We should talk about it."

"How about we go together, you know, just the group? We can talk about the most adult way to handle it."

"If you think that's best," I said, and hung up the phone.

I went to the shops with Jessica. Jessica's dad drove a Volvo and he always made us sit in the back for safety. Jessica's dad was a very serious man. He always played really bad elevator music in the car. If it was my dad I would have forbidden it, but Mr. Chou was not the sort of man of whom you made demands.

Jessica turned toward me and started slowly head-banging in time to the elevator music. She was sitting behind her father, so he couldn't see her. I was trying to stifle a laugh but it came out as a snort.

"Are you all right, Megan?" asked Mr. Chou, looking at me very seriously in the rear-vision mirror.

"I'm fine, thanks," I said, biting hard on the inside of my cheek to keep from laughing.

The group met in the café outside the movie theater and ordered coffees. My mum always said I was too young to drink coffee, but my mum wasn't there.

We took turns talking about our feelings toward Katie Gattrell.

I said that I thought Katie was a very nice person but did honestly think that she was a liability on the net-ball team. It was nothing personal; she just wasn't a good player.

Dara agreed about the netball team, but she still thought Katie should be allowed to be in the group.

Jessica said she had a feeling that Katie was telling other people about our private group business. This was met with a shocked silence.

When Dara asked for evidence, Jessica said a little bird told her and flicked her eyes almost imperceptibly toward me. I don't think anyone else noticed, except for Dara, and she narrowed her eyes. It made me cross, because I hadn't said anything of the sort—not to Jessica, anyway.

Megan Hadenham said that if Katie was telling other people what we were saying, she shouldn't be allowed to be around when we talked about secret group stuff. (Personally, I didn't think Megan Hadenham should be allowed to hear secret group business either—the dirty name stealer.)

Ashley Anderson agreed with all of the above. Candice, as our unofficial leader, abstained. (We were all equal, but Candice was slightly more equal than the rest of us—unofficially, of course—and there were times, in the privacy of my living room, when I was even more equal than Candice, but that was so unofficial that it wasn't even officially unofficial.)

We then had a vote on whether or not Katie Gattrell should remain in the group. Dara was for. Jessica, Megan Hadenham and I were against. Ashley wasn't sure. Candice, as vote counter, abstained.

"You should vote, Ashley," I said. Since everyone else had laid their cards on the table, I didn't think it was fair that Ashley should get out of it.

Ashley looked at Candice with a hunted expression. Poor Ashley. She was so much more comfortable with consensus.

"I think she's nice," she said.

"That's as good as for," said Dara, slapping the table.

"Yes, but, Ashley, is she really group material?" asked Jessica.

"I don't know," said Ashley.

"I think it's a shame we couldn't all agree," I said.

"Why's that?" asked Candice.

"Well, as a group, we should be presenting a united

front," I said. "The very fact that we're having this vote is proof that Katie Gattrell creates a division amongst us. It's not good. Isn't that all the evidence we need? We should have an intervention."

There was an episode of *Seinfeld* where the friends and family of someone who had become addicted to drugs met with the person to explain what a mistake he was making. This was the origin of our "interventions."

They were ambushes. I knew this but it didn't bother me very much, since I'd never been on the receiving end.

We held our interventions in one of the classrooms at lunchtime. The room had beanbags and a fish tank and there were lots of pictures of students on the walls. We liked it because it was quiet. We were allowed to be there unsupervised, and we could intervene without fear of being overheard.

At the end of an intervention, each transgressor was assigned a group member (we called them supporters, but technically they were the equivalent of parole officers) to monitor postintervention behavior.

The interventions worked. Ashley Anderson stopped shoplifting. Dara Drinkwater stopped flirting with Chris Kirkland (which was fair, because diary evidence showed that Megan Hadenham liked him first). Jessica Chou changed her hairstyle.

We had to identify and remove elements that might cause conflict between us. We needed to get these out in the open, deal with them and move on. We all agreed that it was a very adult way to resolve disputes.

Even Candice, who was our unofficial leader, had allowed herself to be interrogated, but only about the subject of her choice—poor academic performance. Candice had been doing very badly around the time she first started going out with Michael.

(Candice pulled me aside beforehand and said that she felt it was important—as unofficial group leader and adjudicator—that she experience the process for herself. I thought this was very noble of her. She asked me to step in on her behalf if it got too heavy, and I promised that I would. After all, she was my very best friend in the whole world and I was sure she would do the same for me.)

The outcome had been that Candice was to sit next to the group member who was the best at each subject, and that person would either coach her or cheat, depending on Candice's level of interest in the subject in question.

I was Candice's supporter for history. Her level of interest was low, and so I did all her assignments for her.

Our group had a secret code. The password was "Do you want to borrow my green pen?"

The green pen was then passed from student to student and when it reached you, you removed the stopper at the base of the pen and there was a note inside where the ink should be.

Katie Gattrell received her summons via the green pen. Of course we didn't call it an intervention in the summons. We just said we wanted to have a chat.

On the third day of detention, Mr. Tilly was our supervisor. I liked Mr. Tilly. He was very short and his big head was mostly bald. He had a round belly and short, stumpy legs. Every day of the year Mr. Tilly wore a short-sleeved shirt with a tie and dress shorts—even in the middle of winter. If it weren't for the baldness, the wrinkles and the enormous cranium, he would have looked very much like a little schoolboy.

Unlike Browney, who always sat in the teacher's chair, Mr. Tilly took one of the students' chairs, turned it around backward and sat astride it at the desk opposite Perdita. "Come and sit over here," he instructed me. I moved over to the desk next to Perdita—not the same desk, but the one next to it.

"So. What have you two been doing in here?" Mr. Tilly asked.

"We have been writing essays about what bad people we are," I replied.

"Aha," said Mr. Tilly, nodding. "And, just between us, do you think you're cured?"

Perdita and I looked at each other. Our eyes met for an instant and then we both looked away.

"I guess so," I said, shrugging.

"Excellent, excellent. We might give the self-flagellation a miss, then, if that's OK with you. So what would you like to do today?" he asked.

I looked at Perdita again, but she was looking down at her lap. "Perdita's pretty good with words," I told him. It was very generous of me, I thought. It showed her that I had noticed something positive about her. I expected her to acknowledge my charity and show some gratitude, but she didn't. Which was very rude, considering who I *was*.

"OK," said Mr. Tilly, rubbing his hands together, "word games. Let me think. How about this: hundred— an overwhelming fear of warlike Asiatic people. Do you get it?"

I frowned and shook my head.

Mr. Tilly held his hands over his face for a moment. "What about . . . what about 'persist: a nasty fluid build-up on a handbag'."

I raised my eyebrow. I had no idea what he was talking about, but he seemed very enthusiastic so I didn't want to put him off.

"Persist—purse cyst. Get it?"

"Oh, I get it," I said, smiling.

"Lieutenant: a person who leases a lavatory," said Perdita, looking up.

"Yes, yes! Exactly!" said Mr. Tilly, pointing at her. "Now your turn, Megan."

I thought for a moment, then shook my head.

"Perdita?"

"Meager: what an ogre calls him- or herself."

Mr. Tilly laughed. "Yes! That's very good, very good indeed." He stood up and grabbed some pieces of paper from the desk, handing a sheet to each of us. "Now we have five minutes. Write down alternative definitions for as many words as you can."

I sat looking at the blank sheet in front of me. Words went through my head. They didn't mean anything except what they already meant. I couldn't do it. It was such a dumb game.

I looked at Mr. Tilly and Perdita. They were both scribbling away.

I let the pen slide along the page and words float through my mind.

Uptight, prospect, mutter, levitate, boastful.

Mr. Tilly looked at his watch, tapped his pen on the table and then leaned back over his paper.

Crouch, mediocre, banquet, mushroom.

Mushroom. Mush-room. A mush room could be a room where something was spilled on the floor. No, that's dumb. Dumb, dumb, dumb.

I couldn't believe I had started this stupid game. That's what you get for trying to be nice to people.

Ostrich, aardvark, antelope. Ant-elope? Anti-lope? That could work.

Boisterous, bottle, bashful.

Bashful—it means shy, but it uses the word "bash," which is the opposite.

I wrote it down.

Mr. Tilly called out, "Time's up. Let's look at what we've got." I handed mine to Mr. Tilly. Perdita paused, tore hers in half horizontally and handed one half to Mr. Tilly. She screwed the other half into a ball and tossed it toward the trash bin across the room. It landed under a desk about two feet short. Perdita would have been terrible at netball.

Mr. Tilly read from our pages aloud. This is what I'd written:

Bashful: aggressive person.

This is what Mr. Tilly had written:

Proceed: a botanist.

Sedate: to look at a calendar.

Understate: Tasmania.

Perdita had written:

Luxurious: describing muscle strain similar to carrying twelve people.

Mr. Tilly read it and looked up at Perdita.

"Lug jury. Get it?" she said. Mr. Tilly smiled and read on.

Acquire: group of people that sing.

Towards: a pair of young people in the care of somebody other than their parents.

Incontinent: traveling overseas for the summer.

Mr. Tilly laughed and rubbed his eyes. "Very good. Very good indeed. Now let's play another. Do you know what a malapropism is?"

I shook my head. Perdita said nothing.

"A malapropism is where you use a word that sounds very much like another word but means something quite different. Let me think. Generality and generosity. Vivacious and voracious, as in 'She had a vivacious appetite.' Do you get it?"

I nodded. Perdita was already writing.

"OK, put them in a sentence. Five minutes. Go!"

Two words that sound the same but mean different things. Comprehensive, comprehend. No, that's not right. They're just different versions of the same word. Ransom, rancid. A king's ransom—a king's rancid. Resemble, assemble, ensemble. A jazz assemble. Better, but not good enough. Nature, nurture. Canopy, canape.

"Time's up," said Mr. Tilly.

This is what I had written:

I served the guests a platter of canopies.

The monkeys lived in the rain forest canape.

Mr. Tilly had written:

The professor gave a fatuous account of the events. It was a long and boorish speech.

"You get two points for that one," said Perdita.

He had a four-wheel drive with a wench on the front.

She was a great tennis player—she was amphibious.

Perdita had put down four sentences:

She asked the doctor for facts but all he would give her was antidotal evidence.

The gentleman was very proud of his lawn of pompous grass.

After a long negotiation, the two businesspeople signed a memoriam of understanding.

I heard that Charles Dickens died of chronicle fatigue.

Mr. Tilly grinned at us both. "Excellent. Most excellent. You are very clever. You've made my day. Now, off you go. See you tomorrow."

I watched Perdita as I was packing my bag. She was smart. I had never thought of her as being smart. I hadn't thought about her at all, really.

I was in all the top classes and Perdita wasn't in any of them. I wondered why that was.

Walking toward the door, I noticed the piece of paper that Perdita had thrown away. I stopped, picked it up and unrolled it. Perdita had written:

Supercilious: Megan Tuw and her friends.

I screwed it up again and threw it into the trash bin, fuming.

7

When I walked into the intervention room on Thursday, Katie Gattrell and Dara Drinkwater were already there. Katie was sitting in one of the beanbags and was already sniveling. Dara had an arm around Katie's shoulder and looked up at me defiantly.

"What have you said?" I asked, standing in front of them with my hands on my hips.

"She asked me, so I told her."

"That's not the way we do it, *Dara*," I said.

"Well, she asked me straight out, *Megan*. You're the one who's always going on about honesty. I told her she couldn't hang out with us anymore."

Katie Gattrell let out a wail and Dara turned back to her and rubbed her shoulder.

Candice, Jessica, Megan Hadenham and Ashley walked into the room behind me. Candice looked at Katie's red, swollen face.

"What's going on?"

"*Dara* has taken it on herself to break the news," I said, raising an eyebrow. Katie was sobbing, holding her face with her hands.

"Well, she asked me," said Dara, shrugging.

Jessica sat down on the other side of Katie and put her arm around Katie's shoulders. Megan Hadenham and Ashley pulled up a beanbag each.

"It's nothing personal, Katie," Jessica began. "It's just that we do stuff like play netball, and well, you're not very . . . It's not that you're not *good* at netball, but we've been playing for longer than you."

"We think you'd be more suited in another group," added Megan Hadenham. "One that does different things. Because, you know how we go shopping? Sometimes we're worried that you might feel bad because you've never got any money. We don't care if you have or not, but we don't want you to feel, you know, as if it matters. So it might be easier on you if you didn't come with us."

Katie was really crying now, and she'd started taking shallow breaths. They were moving too fast. If they kept on like this, she might end up hating us. *Intervention rule number one: Hate is not constructive.* I took over.

"We still want you to be our friend, Katie," I said,

kneeling down. Candice looked at me sharply and I gave her a small nod.

Katie raised her red, teary eyes. "Really?"

"Of course," I said, smiling.

"Oh, I thought you were kicking me out. Dara said you guys didn't want me in the group."

I looked at Dara. She shrugged her shoulders. Dara was such a self-righteous bitch.

"No, don't be silly," I said, patting Katie on the knee.

Katie laughed a small crying laugh of relief.

"But we do need to talk to you about the netball team," I said. "I'm going to be straight with you, Katie. We've been playing for a long time. You've only just started. We think you've got potential. You're much better than Jessica was when she started, isn't that right, Jessica?"

I looked at Jessica and nodded slightly.

"Oh, yeah! I was hopeless," said Jessica, giggling.

"And if you keep practicing you're going to be a really good player," I said.

"Do you think?" asked Katie, looking up at me hopefully and hiccupping.

"Oh, yeah," said Candice, waving her hand, "you could be a real star."

"I'm just being honest with you, Katie, because I respect you, and as a friend I know you'd expect nothing less. Pretty soon you can play for our team. You might even be center one day, but right now you lack experience. It's not your ability, because you do have talent. It's just plain old time on court."

Katie frowned and said, "So if I practice more can I play on your team?"

"Like I said, you could end up being center. Only if you want to. You may find that netball is not your thing, and if that's what you decide, then that's fine too. We'll still care about you. Netball isn't everything."

Katie nodded. "So, can I still come to the games?" she asked.

Dara opened her mouth. "Shut up, Dara," I said sharply. Dara shut her mouth (for once). "Of course you are always welcome to come to our games, but the important thing now is practice, practice, practice, OK? So there's no point wasting time just sitting around watching us play, right?"

Katie nodded.

"So am I still in the group?" she asked. Her voice was quavering.

Candice and I exchanged a glance.

"What's friendship all about, Katie?" I asked.

"Well," she said, thinking for a moment. "Doing stuff together?"

I shook my head. "That's only superficial friendship. Real friendship is in your heart. Real friendship is knowing that you'll be there when you really need each other. Isn't it?"

Dara rolled her eyes. I frowned at her.

"If I were to go away overseas, or change schools, then we mightn't see each other for months, we wouldn't be able to do stuff together, but I would still know that we all cared about each other. I might even make other friends, but that's OK too. It's the same with us here. Just because you're not playing on the net-ball team, or coming shopping, or whatever, doesn't mean we won't be there for each other when we really need to be."

I looked up at Candice.

"Yeah," said Candice, "I have friends that go to other schools. We don't see each other every day but I know they care about me."

"So," Katie started slowly, "can I still hang out with you, then?"

"Of course you can," I said. "But just because we don't spend *all* our time together doesn't mean we're not friends. And if you make other friends, or hang out with other people at school, it doesn't mean we're not still pals, OK?"

Katie smiled and wiped at her cheeks with her hand. "I was really worried," she said. She looked me in the eye. "I thought you guys were kicking me out, and that really hurt, but I'm so glad you've been honest with me, Megan. Now I know we're friends and that means you'd never try to hurt me, or stop me from hanging out with you, doesn't it?"

I opened my mouth and then shut it again.

"Of course," I said.

Katie Gattrell one, Megan nil. She was a much better player than I had thought.

8

Mr. Tilly and Perdita were in the detention room when I walked in that afternoon. Mr. Tilly was sitting in his chair, leaning back with his hands clasped behind his head. I sat at the desk next to Perdita's.

"What form should your redemption take today, do you think?" he asked.

I shrugged. "Whatever," I said with a pout. I was in a bad mood. Katie Gattrell had thwarted me, and after the "supercilious" incident I certainly wasn't going to try to be nice to Perdita again.

"If you don't mind," said Perdita, "we could talk about a poem. If that's all right with you."

This was the very first time that Perdita had volunteered anything. Up to now she had participated, but I thought unwillingly. I stared at her.

"OK," said Mr. Tilly, "what poem would you like to talk about?"

"I've been reading a poem by Yeats. It's called 'A Coat.' May I read it to you?"

Mr. Tilly nodded. Perdita reached into her bag and brought out a dog-eared book. Many of its pages had been turned down and it was bristling with yellow Post-it notes. Perdita flipped through the pages.

She read to us:

> "I made my song a coat
> Covered with embroideries
> Out of old mythologies
> From heel to throat;
> But the fools caught it,
> Wore it in the world's eyes
> As though they'd wrought it.
> Song, let them take it,
> For there's more enterprise
> In walking naked."

When she finished she looked up at us. "Do you think that's true?"

"That depends on what you think it means," said Mr. Tilly.

"Well," she said, "whenever you do something, make something that is of yourself, other people will misinterpret it. So you might as well keep it to yourself."

"I think it means that if you blow your own trumpet then other people will try to get the glory from it as well," I said.

Mr. Tilly leaned forward. "I think it means something a bit different. I think it's about being yourself. I think it means that you don't need fancy-schmancy ways of expressing yourself. You don't need to put on a coat, just be yourself. Read it again."

Perdita read it to us again.

"Do you see? The coat was made of old mythologies. So I think that weaving old ideas in a new way to express yourself leads to the misinterpretation that you were talking about. It's better just to be yourself."

Perdita smiled. "Oh, yeah. I suppose. Thanks, sir."

"You're welcome, Perdita. Any time," said Mr. Tilly.

I looked at their faces. Perdita seemed genuinely grateful for what Mr. Tilly had said, even though it was different from what she thought. She had asked Mr. Tilly a question because she was interested in his answer. It was perplexing. It was new to me.

When we were leaving, I said, "Hey, Perdita, that was a good poem."

"Yeah," she said. Then she picked up her bag and started to walk out.

"It was interesting," I added.

She stopped and looked over her shoulder. "You don't know anything about poetry, Megan."

What was her *problem?* She could have at least acknowledged my effort to be nice—especially considering who I *was.*

9

The next day Candice wrote me a note in maths. She turned to the back page of her book and wrote, *V. imp. group meeting. Need to brief you. Ring you after.*

Candice and I didn't talk in maths. Nobody talked in maths. It must have been really important for Candice to even risk writing me a note. Our teacher was the Denominatrix.

The Denominatrix was the scariest teacher in the school. What was most scary about her was that she didn't look like a monster. She was short and plump and wore her gray hair in a bun at the top of her head.

She looked just like one of the standard grandmothers that you see in kids' books—like the old woman who owned Tweety Bird.

Her face was kindly, with wrinkles facing all the right directions for someone of good nature. Her voice sounded gentle and benign, which was all the more horrifying when she spat venom.

The Denominatrix loved maths and took it as a personal affront when students couldn't do it, or (gasp) didn't like it as much as she did. If you couldn't grasp mathematical concepts in the time the Denominatrix allocated, you were in big trouble.

If you didn't get to class on time, the Denominatrix would lock you out. If you spoke during class without first being spoken to, she would throw you out. If you did anything other than completely understand what she said the first time she said it, you got detention.

She didn't shout or lose her temper, but you were made to feel as though your mathematical ineptitude was some deep character flaw and the best way to address such a dreadful personality blemish was humiliation and then discipline.

Nobody gave the Denominatrix any trouble. Candice and I certainly didn't.

Candice rang me when I got home from detention.

"May I speak to the lady of the house?"

"The lady of the house is speaking."

"To whom is she speaking?"

Then we laughed. We always laughed.

"We have had the most productive group meeting this afternoon while you were on detention. I am so excited. I can't wait to tell you."

"What was it about?"

"Well, you know how all the Year Twelve boys who aren't eighteen yet are going to do the Grand Nudey Run? Well, Michael said that, as a protest, it won't be any good unless people know what we are protesting about, right? So the group has offered to do their PR."

"To do *what*?"

"You know, posters and flyers and stuff."

"Oh." Surely this was a joke.

"You know how I want to do communications—well, I think it will be really impressive on my résumé that I was responsible for a whole campaign so young."

I frowned. "Since when have you wanted to do communications?"

"Oh, for a little while."

This was a bit of a shock to me. I always thought Candice and I told each other everything.

I thought she wanted to be a professional netball player. We had talked about this before. My understanding was that she was going to get a job in an office or a shop or something to support herself while she pursued a sports career. Either that or fashion design. I thought that was what we had agreed.

"How come you didn't tell me?"

"I thought I had. I've been talking about it with Michael."

"You want to do communications and you told Michael before you told me?"

"Oh, stop being such a baby. Anyway, you're not sounding excited enough about the campaign. I feel so strongly about this issue. It's a humanitarian issue, really."

I'm sorry, the "campaign"? "A humanitarian issue"?

"It is?"

"Dara reckons it is."

"Dara would."

"Don't be like that. Dara's good. You should learn to be more tolerant. It's such a shame that you're on detention because that's when we're having our meetings, but I'll ring you straight after and tell you how it's all going."

"Candice, you're not serious about this, are you?"

Candice didn't speak.

"Are you still there?"

"Yeah. Why wouldn't I be serious?"

"Well, it's not a very good idea."

"Megan, I don't think you understand all the issues here."

"No, I don't think I do."

Candice and I were quiet for a moment. We were like two lions meeting at the edge of our territory—standing at a respectful distance, neither of us wanting to take the first step, neither wanting to back down, either.

"Maybe we could talk about this later," she said cautiously.

"Yes. Maybe we should," I said.

I didn't like Candice spending time with Dara Drinkwater. I didn't like her telling me to be more tolerant. They weren't her own words. I could just imagine Dara harping at her when I wasn't there.

It's not me, Candice. I've tried so hard to get along with her. Megan Tuw should be more tolerant.

Yes, they would *all* call me Megan Tuw when I wasn't around. I bet they would.

I didn't like the sound of all these little heart-to-hearts with Michael, either. I had a really bad feeling about this whole Grand Nudey Run "campaign."

10

My dad was really, really loud at netball on Saturday morning—even louder than normal, because he got a parking space right next to the court. It was so embarrassing. He sat in the car and every time I had the ball he tooted the horn and bellowed, "That's my girl!" out the window.

After that we drove up to Novitas. Mum and Dad had bought one of those do-it-yourself log cabins for the property. It was what real estate agents describe as cozy, which meant that one of us had to sleep on the sofa, and that meant me.

We spent the rest of the time outside. Dad was doing

manly chores with power tools and Mum pottered around in the garden.

I alternated between the two of them. It was nice to have each of them to myself. At home the only time that they were apart was when they were busy and didn't have time to talk.

Dad taught me how to change the bits in the hammer drill. He spent a great deal of time talking about "the importance of the right tool for the job." This inevitably led to the "Nothing is more important than time" speech. (This speech was usually accompanied by lots of snapping of fingers. *Snap.* "Gone, just like that." *Dramatic pause.* "Gone." And on this occasion I wasn't disappointed. My dad was so predictable.)

He chastised me about holding the drill by the cord. He was big on preventive maintenance.

My dad is an engineer. He designs adiabatic industrial exhaust systems for manufacturing plants and underground carparks. Whenever we go anywhere, Dad always insists that we stop to look at vents and fans. He can talk about air density for hours. (Mum says it's a gas.)

I helped Mum repot some dracaenas. She talked to me about the importance of having the right balance of tall plants with long spiky leaves and short plants with soft round leaves. She said, "The texture of Novitas isn't visually pleasing," and that this was an upsetting thing.

Mum's speeches were mildly less predictable than

Dad's, but there was always a lot of tut-tutting and Marge-like growls of consternation.

I suggested that for her fiftieth she should ask Dad for fifteen acres in Wichita, Kansas, and then she could replant the whole lot there.

My mother remarked that she was impressed by my knowledge of the climatic conditions of particular states in the U.S. and hoped that I was equally aware of the geography of my own country. I was not, so as a distraction, I offered to make "afternoon tea" (two glasses of red wine, a Coke and some taramasalata on rice crackers).

There was no television at Novitas, so after dinner we played Scrabble. My mother knew too many scientific plant names for the game to be at all fair, so I was allowed to use two colloquial expressions per round (my favorite was "gadzooks") and Dad was allowed to include the surname of one past Canberra Raiders player (one of the books we had at Novitas was *100 Years of Rugby League,* and so his submissions could be cross-referenced).

On the way home we sang Paul Kelly songs in the car. My parents loved to sing "Dumb Things," because when I was little, instead of singing "I've done all the dumb things," I used to sing, "Up and down all the gum trees." Oh, yes. Very amusing.

My favorite song was "Moon in the Bed," because my parents sang the harmonies, and I provided the oooh woohs. It was an excellent driving song.

11

At school, things were a bit tense
between Candice and me, but the only class we had together that day was maths, where we couldn't talk anyway, and Jessica sat between us.

At lunch everyone in the group sat together to eat.
Katie Gattrell was with us too. She sat next to Dara,
who made every effort to include her in the conversation.

Then they started to talk about the stupid Grand
Nudey Run campaign. I listened to them for a short
time, becoming more and more annoyed.

"Michael says people are always being punished for

freedom of expression. It's fascism, that's what it is—fascism," said Candice, pointing her finger at Dara.

Personally, I thought this Jacob guy did a dumb thing and he got caught.

There is nothing fascist about people wearing clothes in public. You could catch a chill, for starters. Also, most of the areas that you're obliged by law to keep covered are rather delicate. You wouldn't want to leave them out in case they accidentally got burnt or scratched or grazed.

"There are so many stupid rules. My dad says the police are all corrupt anyway," said Dara Drinkwater. Dara's father was a property developer. Dara's father said everyone was corrupt. He was always in the newspaper bagging people: *"Clifford Drinkwater calls for inquiry"*: " *'The public deserves to know,' says local business identity Clifford Drinkwater."*

When my mother read these articles she always said that people who develop glass houses shouldn't throw stones, pointing at the full-page ad for Drinkwater & Duncan Developments on the opposite page.

Jessica and Megan Hadenham and I walked across the quad together and then as we reached the door to the library I mumbled something about research and ducked inside. They were so engrossed in Nudey Run talk that they didn't even notice. Typical.

It was a very odd thing for me to do. I had never been to the library the whole time I had been at the school.

I opened the door, and the librarian, whose name was Ms. Gordon and who was therefore referred to as Gordon, Gordon, Library Warden, rushed over to me. I had not even stepped across the foyer before she blocked my path.

I had heard of Gordon, Gordon, Library Warden, but I couldn't remember ever having seen her before. She was very tall, with broad shoulders. She wore a knee-length tartan skirt and a cardigan.

I thought the skirt was probably supposed to be calf-length, but because Gordon, Gordon, Library Warden had disproportionately long legs, she had pulled the waistband up under her bust. I wondered why she had done this, briefly, before her hair distracted me.

Gordon, Gordon, Library Warden must have only had one small mirror. I deduced this from the following evidence: her hair looked all bouffant from the front but from the side it was flat and disheveled—not just a little bit. Gordon, Gordon, Library Warden must have got out of bed that morning, teased her bangs, pulled her skirt right up, looked in her one small mirror and then come straight to work. Nobody who had a full-length mirror would leave the house looking the way she looked.

"Can I help you?" she asked, smiling pleasantly.

"I'm just looking." Which was technically true—looking at very, very bad hair.

"What are you looking for?"

I blinked at her patiently. "A book."

"Which book?"

"I don't know yet. That's why I am looking." I tried to walk past her but she moved in front of me.

"Well, are you looking for a reference book?" she asked.

"Possibly," I said, trying to sidestep.

Gordon, Gordon, Library Warden darted in front of me again. She was right in my face.

"How about you go away and think about the book you want to borrow and come back when you have decided?"

"How about I just go and look at the shelves until I decide what I want?" I said.

"No. I'm very busy. I can't afford the time it might take for you to decide. You go away now and come back later."

Busy doing what, exactly? I was sure there were librarians across the whole country who were flat out, but they were in libraries that people actually went into from time to time. This was the least populated library on the planet. It is quite possible that, somewhere in the desert in the Middle East, there were crypts full of scrolls buried for a thousand years that were more active than this particular library.

Besides, where would I go? I didn't want to sit with the group. I didn't want to sit with any other group. I certainly couldn't sit on my own. I had to come up with something.

I thought of Perdita saying I didn't know anything

about poetry. There I was in a library, with a few minutes to spare. Why not?

"I want a poetry book," I said.

Gordon, Gordon, Library Warden gave me a look that was ten percent surprise, forty percent malice and fifty percent rage.

"Which poetry book?" She pronounced the "wh" so forcefully that my bangs blew up.

"Can't I just look?" I asked.

"No." She stood there in front of me with her hands on her hips.

I was about to argue, but this was clearly going nowhere. I turned around and walked back outside. I thought about walking across the quad back to the group. I changed my mind and walked along the pathway beside the library and around the corner, out of bounds.

There were some really bad Year 10 boys squatting behind the building, smoking.

"Nice tits," one of them said with a leer.

I turned back around the corner again and leaned against the library building wondering what to do. I heard a *"Psst."* I stood up straight, thinking it was one of the really bad Year 10 boys. I was about to walk away when a distinctly feminine voice said, "Megan, up here."

It was Perdita. She was leaning out of the library window above me.

"How did you get in?" I whispered.

"Fire door," she said. "Go around the other side. I'll let you in."

Walking around the back of the building would have been faster, but it meant walking past the really bad Year 10 boys again. I couldn't be certain that I would ever reemerge, except perhaps as little Megan Tuw steaks, so I walked around the front of the building instead. I turned the corner leading into the teachers' car park. Perdita was waiting for me, holding the fire door slightly ajar.

"They can't lock this during the day because it's a fire door," she whispered to me, looking nervously over her shoulder.

"But it doesn't have a handle on the outside," I said.

"Gordon, Gordon, Library Warden gets herself a cup of coffee from the staff common room at exactly nine-twenty-three every morning," whispered Perdita. "I come in here and wedge this door open." She showed me the latch of the door, which had a piece of masking tape over it.

We moved inside and Perdita quietly closed the door behind us.

"What's wrong with her?" I asked.

"You shouldn't have mentioned poetry books," she whispered, smiling.

"Why not?" I asked.

Perdita looked over her shoulder. She shushed me and pushed me down with the palm of her hand on the top of my head, and squatted beside me. "She's coming."

"Who's there?" called out Gordon, Gordon, Library Warden.

I suddenly felt an urge to giggle. I stifled the laugh and covered my mouth with my hand.

"Who's there?" Gordon, Gordon, Library Warden called out again.

Perdita screwed her face up, put her hands on her hips and mouthed the words, *"Who's there?"*

That was the end of me. I scrambled for the door. Perdita was close behind me, holding the back of my school jumper. We sat crouched against the wall of the library and giggled.

The lunch bell rang and we stood up, each letting out an after-laugh sigh. For a moment Perdita didn't look like a freak at all. She looked like just another ordinary girl.

Perdita quietly opened the library door and pulled away the masking tape with her fingernails. The door closed with a click.

"Why shouldn't I mention poetry books?" I asked.

"A few years ago they went missing—about a hundred of them. Mrs. Gordon was severely reprimanded. Now she doesn't let anyone in there at all," Perdita replied.

"Where did they go?" I asked.

Perdita looked at her watch. "You'd better get to class."

Perdita stole them. I bet she did.

"OK," I said. Perdita turned away and started to walk toward the back of the library building.

"Be careful. There are some Year Ten boys lurking there."

Perdita shrugged and then mimed a roundhouse kick and a karate chop, followed by a courteous bow. It was a gesture that could have been supremely dorky, but she managed to pull it off with style.

"Where did the books go?" I asked her again.

"See you here tomorrow and I'll tell you," she said, smiling. Then she disappeared around the corner.

I'd spent about two minutes with Perdita that lunch hour and in that time she had been normal, made a joke and even done a cool karate move. My opinion of her had improved considerably.

12

I turned up to netball on Monday night.
We always have netball on Monday night. We have had
netball on Monday night for years. So I didn't understand why, on this particular Monday night, I was at
the indoor sports center on my own.

I took my phone out of my sports bag and rang
Candice.

"What's going on?" I barked when she answered.

"What?" she replied. You didn't speak to the unofficial group leader that way, even if you were her very
best friend.

"Are you guys running late?" I asked. I knew they
weren't—not all of them on one night.

"Late for what? Oh! I forgot to ring you. Sorry, Meggy. Netball's canceled. We're working on the campaign. I've been so busy, I forgot to tell you."

I didn't say anything for a long time. Candice, *my friend* Candice, would never have forgotten to ring me.

"What do you mean canceled?"

"Dara rang up and forfeited," she said.

Forfeited? Our team had never forfeited.

"And you forgot to tell me?"

"Why don't you come over to my place? You can help with the campaign. There's heaps to do."

"No thanks."

"Don't be such a baby, Megan. Come over. It will be more fun with you here, really."

I didn't want to go to Candice's place and participate in their stupid campaign, but I knew that if I didn't she would just forget how unreasonable she had been, so I went with the full intention of being as sullen and un-cooperative as possible. I wanted her to see how cross I was, then she would be sorry, apologize and give this whole "campaign" business away.

I fumed all the way to Candice's house. I thought about all the little things I had done for her over the years for which she hadn't shown proper gratitude.

Had she forgotten how important netball was for group cohesiveness? This was our *thing*. This is what we did *together*. Forfeited? We *never* forfeited—and all for this stupid, dinky campaign.

I had been to the Perkinses' house hundreds of times

before. It was almost a second home to me. They lived in an old three-story row house. Mrs. Perkins had spent years going around old secondhand furniture stores finding old fittings—door handles, tiles, window frames—to restore it. Mrs. Perkins was very proud of her house.

Whenever I went there she was always showing me a light switch or some piece of molding that I was supposed to be astounded by. When she found an original Kookaburra wood-fired stove she had a drinks party for all her friends. My mother and father went to it.

I couldn't believe what I saw when I walked in. The Perkinses' living room had turned into a workshop. There were rolls of butcher's paper across the floor. There was some girl hunched over a large sheet of material that she was working through Mrs. Perkins's prized old Singer sewing machine next to the dining room table.

Someone was *using* the Singer sewing machine. I remember having been admonished at length for placing a soft-drink glass on that sewing machine for a millisecond.

Ashley and Megan Hadenham were cutting letters out of different material at the other end of the table.

There were people everywhere, people I didn't know but recognized, sewing, cutting and rolling. Katie Gattrell sat laughing between two Year 12 boys. Very cozy.

Candice was walking around between the groups,

pointing with her pen and holding a clipboard. A *clip-board*. Had they all gone *mad*?

I put my bag down in the corner and stood in the doorway waiting for someone to notice me. Nobody did.

A group of Year 11 girls called out to Candice to ask her a question. She walked over to them and knelt down. They all listened intently, nodding and smiling.

Mrs. Perkins was wandering around with a plate of hors d'oeuvres and a handful of napkins. She wandered over to me, offering me a napkin. She was smiling vacuously, and then she recognized my face. "Meggy, I didn't know you were here. Isn't this wonderful? It reminds me so much of my university days. We used to go to protests all the time—well, maybe not all the time, but we did go to a few. They were such fun and *everyone* was there. We were just saying the other day, young people these days—no social conscience—and now look! My little girl. We're so proud."

I made a noncommittal "hmm" noise and took a spinach and cheese triangle.

"It's all vegetarian," Mrs. Perkins said to me, pointing to the plate, "to get into the spirit of things."

Poor Mrs. Perkins. She had no idea what this was about.

Finally, Candice looked up.

"Oh, hello, Meggy," she said. She smiled as if she was genuinely pleased to see me, and my resolve softened, but I didn't let it show. I stood there with my arms folded. I tried to look ninety percent hurt and ten percent hostile. I said nothing.

"Do you want to go out the back?" she asked, slipping her hand around my elbow.

I nodded. *Finally* she was seeing sense. I thought it was important that we sit down and talk this out. There was definitely some group hysteria happening here. I really thought we should talk this through before it went too far.

We picked our way across the paper-strewn floor and toward the back door. Mr. Perkins and Michael Sorrell were at the barbecue, cooking sausages for everybody. "Hey, Meggy, how have you been?" said Mr. Perkins as I walked past. Michael gave me a brief smile.

"Good, thanks, Pa," I replied, smiling brightly.

At the back of Candice's house was a covered outdoor eating area. It had been set up with trestle tables. A group of about eight Year 11 and 12 kids were standing around painting signs and placards.

In the raw against the law, read one.

It's only natural, read another.

"Dara's looking after the painting. She'll tell you what to do," said Candice, and then she turned around and walked back into the house.

My jaw dropped. Excuse me? Taking orders from *Dara Drinkwater*? She had to be joking.

I turned around and followed her. I marched straight past her, picked up my bag (bending at the knees because I was still wearing my netball skirt) and continued marching straight out the door.

"Megan," I heard Candice say to my retreating back. I ignored her and kept walking. She followed me out to the footpath.

"What is your problem?"

I stopped and turned slowly. "*My* problem?"

"Yes," she said, "for the last week you have been acting like a complete bitch. I don't know what's wrong with you. Everybody else is pitching in. Everybody else is having a good time. Everybody else is helping."

"Well, you go in there and have a good time, then, Candice. Obviously our friendship means nothing to you anymore."

"Why are you being like this?" she asked, frowning.

Why was I being like this?

"Like you don't know," I said, to give myself a little bit of time to think about it.

Why was I being like this? Because she was doing this whole campaign thing without consulting me. Because she had taken it upon herself to forfeit our netball game. Because she rang Michael Sorrell more than she rang me. Because she wasn't behaving at all like my very best friend, *and* because this campaign was stupid!

"Because this *campaign* of yours is stupid. It goes against everything we have ever believed in. It's making waves. It's asking for trouble. And for what? For some stupid, drunken Year Twelve guy that you don't even know."

Candice put her hands on her hips and tossed her head. "Well, I'm sorry you feel that way, Megan. And besides, you don't even know what it's about anyway, because you haven't been to any of the meetings." She pointed her finger at me. "For your information, it's about freedom of expression."

I snorted in disgust. Candice always pointed her finger when she was expressing opinions that weren't her own.

"Well, Candice, I suggest you go back inside before I freely express myself."

"I will."

"Good."

"Fine."

Then we turned our backs. Candice stalked back into the house and I marched down the street.

13

I waited all night for Candice to phone
and apologize, but she didn't.

I got dressed for school the next morning, fuming. I
couldn't believe that Candice wasn't prepared to listen
to me, and worse, that everyone else was going along
with her. I would have thought at least one of them
would be on my side. They must be intoxicated by the
attention from the older students, and in particular the
older boys. Of course they were going along with it.

I arrived at school early and sat in the group spot. I
wanted to be there first; that way, if Candice wanted to
avoid me, she would have to go somewhere else.

Candice arrived and sat on the other side of the group, ignoring me completely. Ashley Anderson sat next to me and started talking. She had no idea that there was something wrong between Candice and me.

I talked to Ashley as if she were a long-lost beloved sister. I leaned forward as if what she was saying were the most important thing in the world. I looked over Ashley's shoulder and saw Candice scowling at me. *Ha. Serves you right.*

Katie Gattrell sat with me for a little while. She told me how important this campaign was to her and how wonderful it was to be able to truly contribute to the group in such a meaningful way.

She put her hand on my arm and told me how dreadfully sorry she was that I'd been on detention and couldn't come to the meetings.

"You know, Megan, even if we don't spend time together we still care about you. You told me that once, remember? I have never forgotten what you said to me that day, and I never will," she said with a saccharine smile.

Katie Gattrell two, Megan nil.

I didn't want to sit with the group—with Candice, or Katie—at lunchtime. I decided to meet Perdita at the library instead. But because Perdita was the Freak—the most despised person in the whole school—I had to think up a good story.

Luckily, my class before lunch was geography, and I sat with Ashley. I paid more attention to Ashley that day than I ever had before. She was pretty in a bovine sort of way. She had large, soft, trusting eyes and child-bearing hips. She was an early developer.

Ashley was also the only one in the group who had *done it*. We had an emergency slumber party as soon as we found out, but she just sat there smiling coyly and wouldn't give us any details at all, which I thought was *grossly* unfair.

It was easy enough to use the Jedi Mind Trick on Ashley.

"I have to go to the front office."

"What for?" she asked.

"I have to pay something for Mum."

"Do you want me to come with you?"

"No, you go and have your lunch."

Ashley looked at me with surprise. The group moved in twos or threes. Nobody went anywhere on their own, ever, not even to the toilet. Being alone suggested "no friends," and despite overwhelming evidence that we were indeed very popular, we couldn't at any point in time allow even the remotest possibility of someone thinking we were friendless.

"Are you sure?"

"I'm sure."

"You're really sure?"

These are not the droids you are looking for.

"I'm sure."

I packed my bag and headed toward the administration building. This left Ashley standing in the corridor alone. She looked around warily for a moment and then plodded away back to the herd.

I walked down the corridor with a deliberate spring in my step, my shoulders back and a half-smile on my face, indicating to anyone who might have seen me that I was a confident and clearly very popular young lady making her way to the front office on an errand and that I would be rejoining my companions very shortly.

There was a line outside the office service window. I stood in the line for a while, scrabbling around in the pockets of my bag, so as to look purposeful. If anyone happened to see me and reported back to the group, there was evidence that I had been there.

Outside the administration building was the teachers' car park and across the teachers' car park was the library. Unfortunately, the teachers' car park was very much out of bounds. The only other way to the library was to walk right across the quad in front of everyone and alone. Frankly, I preferred to be caught out of bounds.

I moved out of the line and, settling my bag on my shoulders, I casually pushed open the front door—the one with the sign on it at eye level, TEACHERS AND GUESTS ONLY, NO STUDENTS ALLOWED UNDER ANY CIRCUMSTANCES, EVEN IN CASE OF FIRE, YES THAT MEANS YOU TOO, in big red writing.

I walked across the car park with all the appearance of confidence and purpose, and stopped outside the library fire door. I pushed it open tentatively, my eyes adjusting to the gloom. Perdita was crouched down on the floor reading a book. She snapped it shut and stepped out into the light.

"Come on," she said, and started walking past the cars toward the front gate.

"Where are you going?" I asked.

"Correction, where are *we* going," she said, turning around and walking backward.

"Where are *we* going?" I asked.

"Hurry up," she said.

I looked around and then scurried after her.

"What are you doing?" I said, falling into step with her.

"We're going on an excursion."

Unless I was very much mistaken, we were heading outside the school grounds. I had never cut classes in my life. This was madness. This could get me into trouble. What was I doing? This was the Freak—the most despised creature in the whole school—and I had followed her out of bounds and now *really* out of bounds.

We headed toward the gates and I winced as I walked through them, half expecting some perimeter alert to start blaring and guards to jump out behind the bushes shouting "Freeze!" through loudhailers.

Nothing happened.

We walked along the street silently for a while. I kept looking over my shoulder and I ducked my head every time a car went past.

"Will you stop it? You look guilty," Perdita said.

"I *am* guilty," I retorted.

"Note to self: Megan Tuw has a conscience. It's a small, twisted and deformed one, but it's there."

I was irritated but I let it pass.

We turned left and walked along the narrow path beside the stormwater drain. I relaxed a bit and looked over the tilting wooden fences to the backs of houses. They looked somehow undressed.

Perdita picked up a long stick, holding it like a staff and stabbing it into the ground at intervals.

I bent down to pick up a stick too and suddenly Perdita called out, *"En garde!"* and, hitting my stick with hers, knocked it out of my hand.

"What are you doing?" I asked.

"We're having a sword fight."

"We can't do that. What if somebody sees us?" I said, looking over my shoulder.

"Nobody can see us. Besides, so what if they do?"

I looked around again and, certain that nobody was watching, picked up my stick.

"Are you ready now?" Perdita asked.

"OK."

"En garde," she said, holding her stick up in front of her face. With one hand held dramatically in the air, she lunged toward me.

I had never had a sword fight before so at first I waved the stick about, squealing. I soon got the hang of it, though. It was a bit like hockey—except with sticks raised.

"Mark!" called out Perdita, pressing the tip of her stick against my shoulder.

"Who?" I said, pretending to be looking for someone.

Perdita laughed, leaning on her stick with one hand, the other on her hip. "You wouldn't make a very good musketeer," she said.

"My parents will be heartbroken," I replied.

Perdita's smile disappeared. She dropped her stick and we kept walking. I wondered why she hadn't found that funny.

The stormwater drain was dry. Debris littered the bottom: an old shopping trolley on its side draped in grass clippings, a plank of wood encrusted in mud, a broken bassinet, a stack of cracked black plant pots.

There was a burning issue that I thought we needed to get clear straight away. I've always prided myself on my frankness and honesty. I truly believe that if you are upfront, there's less chance for confusion and less chance for conflict.

So as we were walking I explained to Perdita that I couldn't see her at school. It wasn't that I didn't like her—I did, for sure. It was just that my position in the group made it impossible. Did she understand?

Perdita was watching her feet and her hair had fallen across her face, so I wasn't sure how she was taking it. Still, sometimes you've got to be cruel to be kind, so I continued. I suggested that perhaps she should imagine it like two sporting teams. I was on the green team and she was on the red team. School was like the game:

no matter what we did outside the field, when we were on field we had to play for our own teams.

I talked to her about friendship. I said that real friendship wasn't about doing things together, real friendship was in our hearts, and knowing that we would always be there for each other. I said that just because we didn't spend time together didn't mean we weren't friends. And if I had other friends, or hung out with other people at school, it didn't mean we weren't still pals.

I paused for a moment, waiting for some reaction. There wasn't one, so I went on.

Perhaps she would prefer to think of it like sporting divisions? I was playing in division A and she was in division B, so even if we were playing for the same club, we still weren't playing in the same games.

Perdita said, "Keep your breath to cool your porridge, Kitty."

"What?"

Perdita told me she understood what I was trying to say, and to forget it. She didn't ever want to play for my club. My club was a pack of ostentatious popinjays.

I was surprised. Why wouldn't she want to play for my club? My club was the best club you could possibly play for.

"What's a popinjay?" I asked.

Perdita looked at my shocked face and she *laughed* at me.

14

Perdita lived in the bottom half of a two-story house. It was separate from the top, like a granny flat.

She put her schoolbag down on the ground and opened the door with two hands, turning the key and the handle at the same time.

The room smelt musty and sweet, like incense, like old books. Sunlight, dappled and green, filtered into the room through trees. A row of tiny bells, hung by string from the curtain rail, tinkled in the breeze. Below them was an old desk topped with an arc of tall candles, and small terracotta plant pots filled with pens, colored pencils and paintbrushes. The wooden chair in front of the desk was covered in white daisies painted with Liquid Paper.

I put my bag down inside the door and looked around curiously. The room was clean but untidy. It wasn't like my house. My house looked like a design magazine.

The walls were brick and covered in black-and-white posters, mostly scenes from old movies. The corner of a life-size image of the Alien curled where it had come unstuck from the wall.

In a wooden crate in the corner was a pile of old dolls, dressed in faded old lace dresses, with very pale plastic faces, eyes that blinked and threadbare hair.

There were books everywhere. They were stacked in rows against the walls. A block of books had even been stacked together in the middle of the room, topped with a sheet of Masonite and covered with a piece of lace to serve as a coffee table.

Perdita sat cross-legged on the floor with her back against the wall. I sat on the chair at the desk.

"There are the library books," said Perdita, pointing to the coffee table stack.

"You stole them?" I asked. I knew she had.

Perdita shrugged. "I prefer to think of it as a long-term loan. Besides, nobody else was ever going to read them."

"I was going to," I said.

"Only because I told you to."

"Stealing is stealing is stealing," I said, tossing my head.

"Note to self: Megan Tuw is a pedant," Perdita said to the ceiling. "As if you have taken every book back to school."

"Maybe, but I haven't stolen them intentionally."

"Stealing is stealing is stealing," said Perdita. "Anyway, nobody had ever borrowed any of them for about twenty years. Look at the cards if you want to. Look."

She pulled one of the books out from under the Masonite. She flipped open the cover.

" 'Ellen Wilson, seventh of March 1973.' That's thirty years ago. That's longer than either of us have been alive, and almost as long as both our lives put together. Not a single soul has opened this book between then and now. And look, it's only ever been borrowed twice before that. Once in 1972 and once in 1968."

She snapped the book shut.

"What do you want with them, anyway?" I asked.

"I like poetry."

"What's so great about it?"

Perdita leaned her head against the wall and looked at the ceiling.

"Have you ever felt you were completely alone in the world?"

I thought about it for a moment.

I can remember being very small and going on holidays just with my mother and father. Most days we would do things together as a threesome. We would go to the beach, or we would go to a wildlife park, or on a picnic. But some days my mother and father would put me in day care and go off together.

I can remember crying and begging them to take me along, clawing at their clothing. *Take me with you. Don't leave me here. Don't leave me on my own.*

I can remember the horror of watching them smile and turn away from me. I can remember them physically detaching me from their legs. Leaving me behind screaming and crying. Waving at me from the other side of metal bars. *How could you? Leaving me alone. How could you leave me here? Abandoning me. How could you turn away from your child?*

"Yes. A long time ago," I replied.

"Everything you have ever felt has been felt by someone else," said Perdita. She opened the book again and flipped through the pages.

> *From childhood's hour I have not been*
> *As others were; I have not seen*
> *As others saw; I could not bring*
> *My passions from a common spring.*
> *From the same source I have not taken*
> *My sorrow; I could not awaken*
> *My heart to joy at the same tone;*
> *And all I loved, I loved alone.*

She looked up at me. "Edgar Allan Poe." She closed the book and laid it down beside her.

"Every feeling you have had about anything, ever, somebody has written it. Somebody has captured it. Maybe thirty years ago, maybe five hundred years ago. It's all the same. People are all the same, essentially. Even feeling completely alone—that there is nothing and no one—somebody somewhere has felt it. And when you find a poem like that it makes you feel that you have found a friend. That's what's so great about it."

There was a noise from upstairs. Somebody was coming down. I could hear the gravelly sound of shoes scuffed along concrete, and then the door opened gently.

A woman peered in. She had a gaunt, tired-looking face. She wore no makeup, which made her look pale. Her hair was tied with a rubber band in an untidy ponytail at the back of her head. Her eyes were gray-blue and watery.

"I didn't know you were home," said the woman. Her voice was thick and reedy, as if she suffered from sinusitis.

I tried to think of an excuse for not being at school, but Perdita didn't even bother.

"If you didn't think I was home, then why did you come into my room?" asked Perdita.

If I had spoken to my mother that way I would probably have been sent to my room with no dessert. If my mother had found me at home in the middle of the day, when I should be at school, I would have been flayed; but Mrs. Wiguiggan didn't even flinch.

"I thought I heard a voice, that's all."

She stood in the doorway a moment longer, shifting her weight from one foot to the other. I waited for either of them to say something—anything.

"OK, move along, now. Nothing to see here," said Perdita.

Mrs. Wiguiggan didn't answer—she didn't even blink: she just stood there. Eventually she said, "Well, then," withdrew her head and scuffed away.

We sat listening as she climbed the stairs and then shut the door behind her.

"She's not my *real* mother, you know," said Perdita.

"No?"

That's why she didn't smile when I said, "My parents will be heartbroken" on the way over.

"I'm adopted," she said. She picked up the book beside her and flicked the pages with her thumb. "My real mother is Argentinean. I have her black hair. She called me Perdita."

"Oh?"

"Yes, she had a torrid love affair with an Australian man, an academic—literature. I think he was born here, but his father was South American too. He lived in Buenos Aires for a few years. I think he was studying Jorge Luis Borges. That's where they met. He brought her back here but it didn't work out. So she went back to Argentina, leaving me behind," Perdita said, not looking me in the eye.

I had a very strong image in my mind—a tall woman

with long black hair waving at a little girl from the other side of metal bars. The little girl crying, screaming—little arms outstretched. *How could you? How could you leave me here? How could you turn away from your child?*

"I've never told anyone that before," she said, and then she sighed as though a big weight had been lifted from her.

I shifted in my chair. I felt uncomfortable. I didn't want Perdita to tell me personal things about herself.

I wonder now if telling someone made it feel more real to her—as if she could speak it into being. I wonder if, in her mind, telling me made me responsible for its being true.

15

I turned up at school on Wednesday expecting someone to say something about my disappearing act the day before, but nobody said anything.

Candice and I went for a walk during lunchtime. She asked me if I wanted to go to the canteen and I could see that it was a gesture toward reconciliation, so I agreed.

Ashley was going to come too, but Candice pointedly offered to buy her something and bring it back.

"Let's go this way," she said, heading off toward B block, which was a very circuitous route to the canteen, I thought, but I agreed.

"Things have been a bit strained lately, haven't they?" she said, looking at the ground and avoiding eye contact.

"Yeah, they have a bit," I replied.

"We've been friends for a long time," Candice said.

"We have," I said, sneaking a peek at her face. She was frowning. We walked past a group of Year 7 students sitting in a quiet huddle outside the staff room window.

"Do you remember when we used to sit there?" I said. Candice laughed.

Real estate in the quad moved in a very slow waltz. Every year, when Year 11 moved into the Year 12 common room, the very best positions became available.

Silly Year 7s, who started a day before everyone else, rushed to the best spot for the first two weeks and were quickly exiled, year after year. The Year 8s gladly gave it up. Year 8s were experimenting with swearwords, and sitting outside the staff room is not the greatest place for it.

Groups vied for new positions and those lower in the pecking order got the hottest and windiest spots.

Our group had two of the best spots, better than some of the Year 11s—an indication of our position in the school. We sat on the fixed seats outside the art rooms to eat and then wandered over to sit in a loose semicircle under a tree next to the oval to watch the boys playing sport.

"I think the last time we had a fight was over that stupid pool pony in Year Six," Candice said.

"That's right," I said, smiling at the memory. Candice, red from sunburn and rage, climbed up the steps of our pool, not watching where she was going, and got marooned in a bed of my mother's cacti. She stood there, balanced on one foot, yelling at me. *"You're a . . . a . . . a bad sharer!"*

I yelled back from the pool. *"Oh, yeah? Well, you're a . . . you just stink!"* I had the pool pony but was almost too angry to be able to get on it and half drowned myself in the process.

We had such a long history together. Candice had always backed me up. She had always supported my arguments, no matter how inconsistent, so strongly that even I believed them. We didn't disagree: If there was a difference of opinion, we avoided the subject. We had a very respectful relationship.

We were the group. There were others, but it was the bond that Candice and I had that made the group the unit that it was. People were envious of us. We were smart, funny, pretty: everything you could want to be—everything you needed to be. We were the climate control for the whole year.

"You're a bad sharer," I said.

"You just stink," Candice replied, and we both laughed.

"That was a pretty dumb thing to fight about, hey?" I said.

Candice nodded.

"So are we OK now?" she said.

"We're OK."

Candice put her arm around my shoulder for a moment, shook me gently and then quickly let go. No stupid pool pony or stupid Grand Nudey Run was going to come between us. Everything was OK in Candice and Megan World. For about thirty seconds.

A basketball came bouncing toward us and we stopped, waited for it to pass us and then kept walking.

I thought about telling Candice about Perdita. I wanted to tell her that Perdita wasn't that bad. She wasn't really the freak we had always thought her to be. Perhaps she needed some guidance when it came to clothing, or appropriate behavior, and she couldn't play netball, but she was actually pretty interesting.

I thought Candice would like her, once she got to know her. It might seem odd at first, unnatural maybe, but once you got to know Perdita, she was actually sort of special.

I was just about to tell Candice these things when she spoke.

"So do you want to come over this afternoon? You could stay for dinner," she said.

"Sounds good," I replied. Everything was back to normal.

"Yeah, Dara has nearly finished the painting and the banner will be ready this afternoon. Everyone is coming over to have a look. It's a banner party. We're going to have a barbecue."

• • •

In the interests of peace and harmony I went to the stupid banner party. I stood in the middle of the group laughing at their stupid in-jokes that I didn't get because I hadn't been there. I watched them all flirting with boys that I didn't know, and having earnest, intimate discussions with older girls I had seen but never spoken to.

Candice was the belle of the ball. She flitted from one group to the next, holding people intimately by the forearm, organizing drinks, leaning forward conspiratorially. Candice was *everybody*'s best friend.

She sat on the edge of a chair next to a Year 12 girl. They were talking and laughing. Candice stood up, patted her on the shoulder and said, "Ring me after, OK? Promise?"

I saw Candice standing in the corner with Katie Gattrell—*Katie Gattrell*—whispering. She turned her head to the side so that Katie could whisper in her ear. I saw her look over Katie Gattrell's shoulder, and with a wicked little grin, she winked at Dara Drinkwater.

I watched her from my place on the Perkinses' designer outdoor chair. Had she outgrown me? Had we outgrown each other? Was she just punishing me over this stupid campaign business?

I ate chicken kebabs and potato salad from a paper plate balanced on my knee and drank a soft drink from a plastic cup.

Katie Gattrell came to sit with me for a while. She confided in me that she didn't think she would ever be good enough for our netball team.

"I know you said if I practiced I would get better. You said I had talent, but I think you were just being nice. You also said netball wasn't everything, remember? And now look, here we are doing the campaign instead. So you were right."

Katie Gattrell three, Megan nil.

"I wouldn't hang up my boots just yet if I were you, Katie. The campaign will be history next week and then you'll be back on the bench."

Katie Gattrell three, Megan one. I was making a comeback.

I mingled, blended, manufactured enthusiasm and didn't draw attention to myself in any way until the dramatic unfurling of the stupid campaign banner. There it was in big, bright, meter-high letters: SAVE JABOC.

I was the only one who laughed. An uncomfortable silence followed.

16

On Thursday I left the house, ready to go to school, and there was Perdita sitting in the gutter just around the corner from my house with her elbows hooked around her knees, squinting in the sunshine. She was wearing high-waisted jeans that were too long for her, rolled at the cuffs, and a faded gray long-sleeved shirt. Nobody wore their jeans like that.

When she saw me she stood, pulling the strap of her old tattered bag over her head and onto her shoulder.

"What are you doing?" I asked.

"Correction—what are *we* doing?"

I frowned. It annoyed me that she had made an

assumption about what I was and wasn't going to do. I let it slide.

"What are *we* doing, then?" I asked.

"We're going on an excursion."

"Where to?"

"Somewhere better than school."

Then she turned and started to walk along the street. After a moment she turned around.

"What?" she asked impatiently.

"I'm supposed to be going to school."

She put one hand on her hip. "I promise you'll come home a wiser person. OK?"

I stood still.

She sighed. "Note to self: always remember to pander to Megan's insatiable ego. Will you please come with me today, Megan, because I enjoy your company above all things and it will be a dull and empty day without you?"

I cocked my head to one side. "I am willing to consider a bribe."

"That's an ugly, ugly word."

"How about a sponsorship arrangement?"

"Too capitalistic. Let's call it a subsidy."

"I don't need charity. Perhaps we could negotiate an incentive?"

"Whatever. What's your price?"

I thought about it for a second. "A dozen donuts."

"I will buy you a dozen donuts just as soon as an appropriate donut vendor can be found. Now, come *on*."

We caught the train to Central Station. True to her word, she bought me a dozen donuts from a takeaway shop on Pitt Street.

I munched on them, occasionally holding open the paper bag for Perdita, as we walked up Broadway.

"You know, you should get some hipsters," I said to her.

"Some what?"

"Hipster jeans."

"Why?"

"Because the ones you've got on have a high waist. Nobody wears them like that," I explained.

Perdita looked down at her jeans as she walked.

"They cover my arse, what does it matter where the waist is?" she said.

What did it matter, really? I know I wouldn't have stepped outside my front door in the jeans she was wearing. Why was that? Because if I did, I would look different from everyone else. Because people would laugh at me.

I watched Perdita as she clomped along with her chin jutting out and her shoulders stooped. Perdita didn't care about people laughing at her.

I shrugged. "That's just how people are wearing them now."

"You mean how *your* club wears them?" she asked.

I frowned and looked away. She made me cross. I didn't laugh at the things that were important to her. I didn't tease her about her poetry.

"Where are we going?" I said, changing the subject.

"You'll see," she replied.

We walked across the lawn of the university and through a tall archway. Perdita marched along the sandstone walkways and through the labyrinth of buildings and staircases with purpose. Conspicuous in my school uniform, I felt like a trespasser. Perdita walked around as if she belonged there.

Eventually we stopped in front of a door. Perdita opened it quietly and we stepped into the back of the room.

I had been to a university before with my mother, but never to a real live lecture. A few of the students turned around as we entered. I tugged uncomfortably at my skirt.

Perdita and I sat in two seats at the very back of the theater. The lecturer looked up at us for a moment and then he continued speaking, pacing up and down at the front, swapping a whiteboard marker from one hand to the other.

"While the specific experiences of a particular writer are going to have a great impact on his or her work, it is important not to forget the broader context, lest we fall into the trap of judging the work by our own social standards. And so I say, at the risk of enraging the feminists in the room, if you're looking for context, study the 1940s and 1950s, don't study Ted."

Perdita quietly got out a pad and a pen. She wrote and then slid the pad across so that I could read it.

That's my father.

I took the pad and pen and wrote back.

Ted?

No, silly. He's talking about Ted Hughes—Sylvia Plath's husband. I mean him. Professor Sabio.

I looked up at the professor, searching for physical similarities. He didn't have Perdita's walk. He was much more graceful. He stood quite tall, with his shoulders back. There was something lithe and athletic about him.

I watched him as he spoke. He seemed very calm and composed, his voice carrying easily across the wide expanse.

". . . Above all, I encourage you not to get lost in context. Context is important only insofar as it helps us to appreciate the work. I will not be handing out high marks for your ability to remember dates, nor for that matter, the names of Plath's various pets. If you want to get lost, get lost in the work itself."

Perhaps there was something about his jawline, his facial bone structure that was similar to Perdita's? Maybe it was the way he turned his head as he was speaking that I recognized?

"I thank you all for your attention. You have your reading lists. I encourage you to read 'The Thin People' before the next tutorial," he said, and then gave a little bow.

Perdita and I picked up our bags and walked out into the sunshine.

"Don't you want to say hello or something?" I asked.

"What do you mean?" she said.

"To your dad."

Perdita crossed her arms over her chest and started walking along the path. "He doesn't know."

I walked along beside her, watching my feet.

"That's why I came here in the first place. I wanted to talk to him—get to know him. I sat in on a lecture. He talked the whole time and I got to hear his opinions about poetry and other things. So I came back and then I came back again, and pretty soon I was here every week. I don't have to tell him. I sort of know him already."

"But don't you want him to know you?"

"He does know me. I go to his tutorials as well. They're good. You should come to one of those, too."

We walked into the cafeteria. Perdita ordered two coffees and we sat at a table near the window.

"But wouldn't he recognize your name?" I asked.

"Why would he?"

"I thought you said your mother named you," I said. "Perdita isn't very common."

Perdita spooned some of the froth from her coffee. "Yes, but they would have broken up by then. I don't think he would have let me be adopted if he had known. He would probably have thought that my mother took me back to Argentina with her."

I nodded and drank my coffee. I'd assumed that

Perdita had known her mother. I had imagined that she'd been part of her own family unit and that she remembered it. What she told me made the story sadder. At least in my version she would have had some happy memories.

"Are you going to tell him?" I asked.

"Maybe one day," she said. "At the moment I can see him a couple of times a week. He talks to me and there are no complications. If I tell him, it might change the way he thinks about me. He might act differently."

I watched Perdita sitting opposite me and stirring her coffee. We were very different people.

My dad had always been there as long as I could remember and I had never had any reason to consider that he wouldn't be there forever. I couldn't possibly imagine what my life would be like without him.

"I think you should tell him. If it was me, and I had a child, I'd want to know them."

Perdita had her elbows on the table and was holding her coffee cup in two hands. "You don't know shit, Megan."

"I know enough not to insult people when they are only trying to be helpful," I retorted.

"I wasn't asking for your help."

I put my cup down and picked up my bag. I wasn't going to stay there while she abused me.

"Where are you going?"

"I'm going home."

"Don't be like that. Relationships are complicated. You've lived your whole life in a shrink-wrapped world. That's not your fault. Just don't try to tell people how their world is, OK?"

I wavered for a moment.

"What would you tell him if you could?"

"What do you mean?"

"Maybe you could write him a letter or something?"

Perdita slid my notepad across the table in front of her.

"Dear Professor Sabio," she said as she wrote, "I think you are my father. Regards, Perdita."

"Aren't you going to put in something else?" I asked.

"Like what?"

"I don't know, something a bit warmer. Maybe about how you like poetry? Maybe you could write it as a poem?" I suggested.

Perdita tore off the page and screwed it up in a ball.

"Dear Professor Sabio, when all is ill and life's no thrill and takes a heavy toll, poetry is what there is to soothe my troubled soul. By the way I think you might be my father. Kindest regards, Perdita."

I shook my head. "You're a dill."

"What?" she said, smiling.

"Be *serious*."

Perdita tore off the page and began to write, fast. When she'd finished, she handed me the paper.

What is at the core? What is the essence on which the soul sups? I whisper verse words. When I speak it, it is gruel, the life-sustaining intravenous drip, the junkie's hit. But who is he who speaketh the songs of the soul and makes it live? My father. Perdita Wiguiggan.

"That's really good," I said, smiling at her.

She shrugged. "So, do you want to come to the tutorial?"

"Will I have to cut school again?"

"No, it's at night."

"Then we should have a sleepover afterward!" I jumped in.

A rash suggestion, as it turned out.

17

Candice rang when I got home. My mother came into my room with the phone. She had her hand over the mouthpiece.

"Candice was wondering how you were feeling. She said you weren't at school today." She handed me the receiver. "I think we should have a little chat, don't you?"

I took the phone from her.

"Hi there," I said.

"Are you sick?" Candice asked. She knew I wasn't. I could tell by her voice that she knew.

"I've got a little bit of a flu, I think," I lied.

There was a pause. I could hear Mrs. Perkins cleaning up in the kitchen behind her. Mrs. Perkins always washed the dishes before she put them in the dishwasher. I remembered one time I had made a joke about it. Candice had looked at me deadpan. "Well, the dishwasher doesn't remove everything, you know," she had said. I learned a lesson that day. Never pay out other people's mothers, no matter how silly their behavior seems.

"Look, Megan, is this about last night? I know I didn't talk to you much. It's just that there were so many people there."

"Don't worry about it."

"I've just been so wrapped up in this whole campaign business. We haven't spent much time together."

"It's OK."

"No. I want to know what you really think. You seem to have some reservations about it. You're my friend and I should hear you out."

This was *long* overdue as far as I was concerned.

I took a deep breath. "Well, I'm not opposed to protest. I think if there is an injustice, we should protest. I believe in the stronger protecting the weaker, really I do. It's just that I see no injustice here."

Candice said nothing, so I continued. "There are so many good things to protest about—hunger, homelessness, poverty, animal rights and so on. I just think this is a dumb thing to protest about."

"What about freedom of expression?" asked Candice.

"Then hold a protest about the truly oppressed people, people who are locked up for expressing their political beliefs, or for practicing their chosen religion. I don't think Jacob was trying to express himself. Do you? Really? I think he was just drunk."

Candice paused and then said quietly, "Well, it's on this Saturday. What do you think I should do?"

"I think you should cancel."

"But I don't think I can cancel. Everyone is all worked up about it. We've got about fifty people coming."

"You asked for my opinion and I've given it. You do what you think is the right thing."

"Thanks, Megan."

"No prob, Bob," I said, smiling.

"Now," she said, "where did you really go today?"

I thought about it for a moment. *Well, Candice, I spent the day with the Freak.* What would she say? On the other hand, this was Candice, my very best friend in the whole world. We had no secrets.

"I went to Sydney University."

"What for?"

I paused. *Should I tell her?* I had to trust my instinct. Candice knew I was up to something. You can't be friends with someone for so long and not know that something was going on.

"I went with Perdita Wiguiggan."

I don't think Candice could have been more surprised.

"The *Freak*? Why?"

"Well, she was on detention with me. I sort of got to know her a bit. She's . . . she's different when you get to know her."

"Oh, *Megan*."

"No, Candice. You don't understand. She's smart. I didn't believe it either at first. You should meet her. I think you'd like her."

I listened to the words coming out of my mouth. *No, she wouldn't.* Candice wouldn't like her at all. There were no two people who had less in common than Candice and Perdita. There were no two value systems on the planet more opposed than those belonging to Candice and Perdita. Candice would never be able to see beyond Perdita's high-waisted jeans.

I had made a mistake. This was the Freak I was talking about—the Freak. That first day she'd approached me in detention I'd held my breath, as if just by standing near her I could get some sort of disease. Why would Candice behave any differently?

Candice was the unofficial leader of the group. Perdita was the most despised creature in the whole school. It was like ice cream on a meat pie, or an onion milk shake. It was just *wrong*.

What was I thinking? I had to backtrack fast.

"She's having a bit of a rough time. It was just a one-off, really. She needed someone to go with, and I said I would. That's all."

"You *spoke* to her? Why were you speaking to her?"

"Only a few times."

"Oh, Megan. You're not going to see her *again,* are you?"

I paused. What about the sleepover? "No. Of course not," I lied.

"Are you sure?"

"Yes."

"Good." Candice took a deep breath. "I think we should keep this between ourselves, don't you? I mean, I understand totally, you were just helping the Freak out, right? That shows compassion. I can see that, but the others won't understand. You do realize that if this got out, it would be the end of the group. *Nobody* would respect us."

"Sure. It really was just a one-off, I swear."

I hung up the phone and lay down on my bed, putting the pillow over my head. I groaned. What had I done? Candice was right. Nobody would respect us. I was consorting with the Freak. Had anyone seen me?

I rolled over. My mother was standing in the doorway with her arms folded.

"Would you like to tell me what's going on?"

"It's a long story."

"I guess I should sit down, then. Do you want to start from the beginning?"

I thought about telling Mum the whole story, but there was no way she would understand.

"I cut school today, Mum. I swear, it was the first

time ever. I made a big mistake, but everything's back to normal now."

My mother nodded slowly. "Are you sure there's not more to it?"

"There is, but I'll sort it, OK?"

"We don't want you to keep things from us, darling. We will love you whatever you do."

She was looking concerned. I could just see the images forming in her mind: drugs, binge drinking, underage sex.

"It's not what you think. It's a stupid thing, really."

"Well, what?"

"OK, OK. Candice doesn't like me being friends with Perdita. That's all."

My mother smiled. She was relieved. Just a bit of petty jealousy, that was all. "It seems to me this Perdita girl needs you far more than Candice does," she said, patting me on the leg.

Poor Mum. She didn't understand anything.

18

There was a feeling of dread in my stomach as I got ready for school in the morning. Every time I thought about seeing Candice I shuddered with embarrassment, and something else—fear.

Candice knew something terrible about me. Before now we had always conspired together. Now Candice had something over me and I had nothing. I just had to trust her.

Candice was my very best friend in the world. It was Candice who had suggested that we keep it to ourselves, wasn't it? If I had been anyone else she would have called an intervention on the spot. We'd held an intervention over Jessica Chou's *hair,* for heaven's sake.

But what if it slipped out? What if somebody had seen me? That would be the end.

I looked at myself in the mirror. "This is a brand-new day, Megan Tuw," I said to my reflection.

Besides, I had made it quite clear to Perdita that we could never really be friends. She knew her position in the school as I knew mine. Yesterday had been wrong. It had been a mistake, but today was a brand-new day.

I walked into school with my confident and purposeful face on. I would know in an instant if something was off. I would see it in their faces. What would I do? I could run away. I could go to the sick bay. I could walk out of the school, go straight home and never come back.

I turned the corner. They were standing together in a huddle. Were they talking about me?

Then Jessica waved to me with a big cheerful grin. "Meggy!" she said.

There now, everything was OK. Everything was fine.

I sat down next to Jessica. She babbled away happily, updating me on yesterday's events.

What was I so worried about? How dumb was I? These people loved me. These people were my friends. Everything was fine.

It may have been my imagination or my guilty conscience, but there was something funny about Dara Drinkwater on that Friday. She kept bringing up my absence.

"So where did you get this flu from, Megan? Or,

should I say who? Look, you're all flushed. Better not sit too close, Megan, you wouldn't want to give your germs to the rest of us."

If I didn't know better, if I didn't trust Candice—my best buddy—I would have thought Dara knew. But Candice couldn't have told her. She wouldn't have told her.

After lunch the worst thing that could have happened, happened. I was walking along the corridor between Jessica and Megan Hadenham when I felt a tap on my shoulder. I turned around. It was Perdita.

"What do you think you're doing?" I said, quickly turning back around again.

"I just wanted to know what time you are going to come over," she said.

"I can't talk to you here," I said, quickly over my shoulder.

Just then Megan Hadenham turned around and started to shriek. "Oooh! The Freak! The Freak! Get away from us."

Perdita looked Megan up and down and then said to me, "Why do you value these people?"

I kept walking. "Go away," I said over my shoulder.

Megan Hadenham was still screeching. She put her hands over her nose and mouth. "Get it away from me! Get it away!"

"Shut up, would you, Megan," I said.

Megan closed her mouth, looking at me with surprised eyes.

"Just go away, Perdita," I said.

Jessica linked her arm in mine. "Yeah, keep away from our friend, you nutcase," she said, dragging me down the corridor.

Perdita shrugged, stopped walking and disappeared in the flow of students in the corridor.

"What was all that about?" asked Jessica.

"Search me," I said.

"She was talking as though she knows you," said Jessica. "What a nutcase."

We spilled out of the doors and into the quad with the other students. Ashley and Candice were already at our seats.

"Guess what?" said Jessica, sitting down with the others. "The Freak just accosted us in the corridor."

"What did she say?" asked Ashley.

"I don't know, she was just babbling. You know what she's like," I said, sitting down.

"I think she was asking you to go somewhere with her, wasn't she?" asked Jessica. "Did you hear what she said?"

"I don't know what she was talking about," I said.

Candice looked at me with narrowed eyes. I was so glad it had been Jessica there in the corridor and not Dara Drinkwater. Dara would have recognized our familiarity in an instant.

I got my drink out of my bag and took a swig. "So, tomorrow's the big day, isn't it? How's it going?"

Just then Katie and Dara walked up and put their bags down. I willed Jessica to let it lie. She didn't.

"Guess what? The weirdest thing just happened," said Jessica. "The Freak just walked up in the middle of the corridor and talked to Megan Tuw like she knew her. We're just trying to figure out what she was trying to say."

"Really?" said Dara, smiling. "Why would she do a thing like that, do you think?"

She knew. I could see it in her face.

I looked at Candice. Candice avoided my eyes. Dara *knew* because Candice had told her. Ms. Let's-Keep-It-Between-Ourselves Perkins had told her. I couldn't believe it.

"Why would she do a thing like that, *Megan*?" Dara asked again.

"I don't know, *Dara*," I said. "Does it matter?"

"Of course it matters. Why would she single you out, do you think?"

"If you're so interested, why don't you go and ask her?"

"I will. I think we should get to the bottom of this, don't you?" she said, and she started to walk away.

I froze. I thought about trying to stop her, but that was exactly what Dara wanted me to do. She didn't want to expose me, she wanted me to expose myself. I suspected that Candice had her on a short leash. She wasn't supposed to know.

The others sat there perplexed as they watched her walk away. Jessica looked at me with questioning eyes. I shrugged.

Dara wouldn't be able to find her. She wouldn't have any more luck getting past Gordon, Gordon, Library Warden than I had. And if she did see Perdita in the playground she wouldn't walk up to her, not with the whole school watching.

Nobody was going with her. Dara was on her own in this particular crusade. Even if she came back with something to report, nobody would believe her. Who would believe that I was fraternizing with the Freak?

"Dara, come back," said Candice. "It doesn't matter. Megan is safe now she's with us."

I didn't feel very safe.

Dara came back grinning. She laughed it off as if it were just a big joke. Oh, yes. Very funny.

They are always with us, the thin people
Meager of dimension as the gray people

On a movie-screen. They
Are unreal, we say:

It was only in a movie, it was only
In a war making evil headlines when we

Were small that they famished and
Grew so lean and would not round

Out their stalky limbs again though peace
Plumped the bellies of the mice

Under the meanest table.
It was during the long hunger-battle

They found their talent to persevere
In thinness, to come, later,

Into our bad dreams, their menace
Not guns, not abuses,
But a thin silence.
Wrapped in flea-ridden donkey skins,

Empty of complaint, forever
Drinking vinegar from tin cups: they wore

The insufferable nimbus of the lot-drawn
Scapegoat. But so thin,

So weedy a race could not remain in dreams,
Could not remain outlandish victims

Sylvia Plath, "The Thin People" (excerpt)

The night of the tutorial, Mum and Dad

were going out. I was anxious about being with Perdita again, but a bit rebellious about the group and its rules. Besides, I had it all planned. We would be going straight to the university and straight back to Perdita's house, so nobody would see us. Nobody knew where she lived. It wasn't the side of town that my friends ever went to, anyway. It would be safe. It would be just one night, and then I could avoid Perdita after that.

Before I left, I put Perdita's letter in an envelope and

left it on the kitchen bench with the other letters that Mum was going to post. I addressed it "Professor E. Sabio, University of Sydney." I didn't know whether or not it would get to him. I left it up to Fate.

I knocked at Perdita's door and stood looking out at the garden while I waited.

Despite my anxiety, I thought it would be fun, going to university at night, like an adult. There was no harm in going to one tutorial. Nobody would see me.

I heard the door squeak as it opened behind me.

"What do you want?" Perdita asked.

"Are we going to this tutorial, then?" I asked, turning.

Perdita stared at me for a moment. Her expression was sixty percent offended and forty percent annoyed. "What, you can talk to me now?"

"Yeah, that's right."

We stood there in silence for a moment.

I put my hands on my hips. "Look, I told you upfront how it was going to be. School is the game, and so on. You said you didn't care. You said you didn't want to play for my club, remember?"

Perdita frowned. I couldn't see why *she* was being snooty. I was the one who should be cross, after her little stunt.

"I can just turn around and we can forget the whole thing if you want," I said, taking a step backward. It would have been a relief.

Just for a moment Perdita looked desperate and sad,

and I felt bad for her. I was the only team she had. As far as I knew, the only team she had *ever* had.

"Mum said she would drive us. Are we going or what?" I said gruffly.

Perdita stepped outside, shutting the door behind her.

"Aren't you going to tell your mum where you're going?" I asked.

"She's not my mum."

We climbed into the car and I made the introductions.

"So, what do you do, Mrs. Tuw?"

"Please, call me Eileen. I'm a botanist. I specialize in succulents."

Perdita smiled. *"Shadow for the sand rat, spines / And barbary ribs clenched with green wax. / Seven thousand thorns, each a water slide, / A wooden tongue licking the air dry."*

"That's lovely," said my mother, looking at Perdita in the rear-vision mirror. "Who wrote that?"

"An American poet called Pattiann Rogers."

"I haven't heard of her before," said my mother.

"She's fairly new to the scene. She wrote that in about 1993 or 1994, I think."

My mother sighed. "I stopped reading poetry such a long time ago. You tend to think of poetry as something old. Fifty years from now, students will probably be studying Rogers, and here we are living in her time and not knowing a thing about her. I really should catch up."

"Why don't you come with us?" suggested Perdita.

"Thanks, Perdita, but maybe another time. Megan's father is taking me out for dinner."

Mum dropped us off on the corner outside the Broadway shopping center.

"If the two of you were dressed differently I might have suspected that you were going to some nightclub, but you seem to be genuine. I'm very impressed," she said.

Perdita and I arrived late for the tutorial. Perdita quietly pushed the door open. A group of about fifteen students were sitting around in a haphazard semicircle. They all turned toward us. Professor Sabio, standing at the front, pointed to two chairs at the right-hand side, then turned his attention back to a pale man who was speaking.

". . . so when she uses the expression 'donkey skins'— beasts of burden—I think she is talking about an underclass, and not specifically about Jewish people. I think the reference to wrapping themselves in the skins and the cups of vinegar suggest that it's their own fault. No perpetrator is referred to, so there is resentment there."

"Thanks for that, Lars," said the professor. He turned to Perdita. "You're late." He looked at his watch. "Very late."

"Sorry," she said sheepishly.

"Well, I expect you'll make up for it," he said, giving her a warm smile. "Who's this?" He pointed to me.

I felt all the eyes in the room turn toward me. I slid down in my chair, trying not to be noticed.

"This is Megan," said Perdita.

"Hello, Megan," said the professor. "I'm Professor Sabio. You'll get to know the other students' names as we go along. How familiar are you with the work of Plath?"

"I'm not," I said. There was an uncomfortable silence. Professor Sabio looked down at his notes for a moment.

"Let me summarize. Sylvia Plath was a poet. She was popular at school, gifted academically, but she was not a happy camper, nor averse to telling the world so. She wrote hundreds of poems—all of them gloomy. She gassed herself when she was thirty. We are looking at her poem 'The Thin People' today. I have a copy of it here." He passed a sheet of paper to a girl at the front, who passed it back over her shoulder to me.

"If you would like to take a moment to read it, we'll continue with our discussion." He gave me a quick but dismissive smile.

"Rita, what do you think?" he asked, pointing to the girl at the front.

"I think Lars is partially right. I think it's about the guilt we feel when we look at victims who have survived. If people die we can feel sorrow, but when victims survive we have to live with the guilt of our own good fortune. For as long as they live, they are a constant reminder. For example, look at the lines, '... when we/were small that they famished and / Grew so lean and would not round / Out their stalky limbs again. ...' The Holocaust is an easy reference point, but in this poem I think it is a metaphor for the same enforced guilt in everyday life and there is definitely resentment, even contempt. Possibly the guilt she felt about her own middle-class upbringing."

Others around the room nodded.

"That's certainly one interpretation. Autobiographical elements appear throughout her work," said Professor Sabio.

Perdita leaned forward in her seat and spoke. "It's too easy to assume that all her poems are autobiographical. Writers imagine, and their imaginings will be shaped by their experiences. People are always looking for some connection between a writer's writing and her 'real' life. I think we should recognize that there is a relationship, but look further than Plath's own life to find answers."

"Good point, Perdita," said the professor. "Megan, keeping in mind that you've only had a cursory glance, what do you think Plath was trying to say?"

Here's where I tried to be clever. I piped up when I should have shut up.

I said, "Well, a lot of people are really jealous of thin people, especially in the movies, so maybe she was jealous of them, you know, for being thin."

There was a long, uncomfortable silence. I felt myself going red. The others were looking at their notes. One student cleared his throat. I looked at Perdita sitting next to me. Her face was blank.

If I had been even partially on track, Professor Sabio might have tried to save me. He might have said, "I think what you're trying to say is . . . ," followed by something even mildly close. Instead, he shifted the attention as far away from my comment as he could.

"Some people would argue that she is also referring here to a thinness of character, or spirit. She refers to a lack of color, a grayness. Would anyone like to comment on that?"

I was embarrassed and ashamed.

I felt humiliated. I knew I didn't belong there. I hated every one of them. Who were they to patronize me? I was only sixteen. I'd never read any Sylvia Plath until ten minutes ago, and all of a sudden I'm supposed to be an expert?

A lot of people *are* jealous of thin people. They are in *my* world!

So I sat there feeling extremely hostile—feeling exactly the way that Perdita must have felt every day at school, a spectacle for the peanut-crunching crowd.

20

As soon as we arrived back at Perdita's I felt a wrongness. The minute I stepped into the room I felt my hair stand on end. The muscles across my shoulders grew tense.

There was movement upstairs. We both looked at the ceiling. Thump, thump, thump and then a long period of silence. Perdita glanced at me with wide and nervous eyes. Something was happening upstairs. No voices—just indistinguishable, erratic movement.

I put my bag down and sat cross-legged on the floor. Perdita sat at right angles to me, leaning her back against the bed.

After another thump, Perdita leapt up to put on some

music. When she stood I jerked, startled. We looked at each other. Under different circumstances we might have laughed, but we didn't. We just pretended it hadn't happened.

Perdita squatted down on her heels in front of her old tape deck and sifted through the tapes that were piled next to it. She selected quickly and pressed Play. She played a whole range of music that night—Grieg, Dvorák, the Breeders—but it didn't disguise the muffled thump, thump of footfalls upstairs.

In a short pause between Slavonic dances I distinctly heard the sound of a slap and then a muffled grunt. It was so fleeting that it was very easy for me to imagine that I hadn't heard it at all, and that's exactly what I did.

We didn't talk about what was happening. We didn't talk about the tutorial. We played music instead. Perdita inserted one tape after another, not waiting for one to finish before the next. We talked about anything we could think of, other than what we were hearing, in louder and louder voices.

I talked for a long time about Novitas, which on reflection was probably unkind of me. To me it was a comfort to talk about the place where the sun always seemed to be shining and the only scuffling to be heard was purely intellectual.

I missed my parents, and if they hadn't been out, I would have phoned them and asked them to pick me up.

I can't remember what we said. I can only remember trying really hard to unhear the noises from upstairs. I unheard for hours and hours.

At about two in the morning, Perdita turned the tape player off. She sat still for a moment looking at the floor and frowning. She seemed to be concentrating but I think she was listening for any residual sounds—making sure that whatever had been happening was over.

"Time for bed," she said. She rolled out a trundle bed from under her own and quickly made it up with linen from her cupboard. We changed into pajamas with our backs turned to each other, and then she turned out the bedside lamp.

I lay on my back with my hand behind my head, letting my eyes adjust to the darkness.

"Perdita?"

"What?"

"I've been thinking about what I said in the tutorial and it was dumb."

She didn't reply. She just shifted underneath the covers.

I started to explain. "I could have said something else if I'd had time to think about it—"

Perdita interrupted. "It's not important."

I lay awake for a while, waiting for her to speak. Every sleepover I had ever been to in my life I had talked almost until dawn. Talking till dawn is what sleepovers are for. If you were really going to go to sleep, you might as well get your mum to pick you up late.

This sleepover was different. I don't know what happened at Perdita's house that night but I can guess. There was something terrible happening upstairs.

I've thought about that night a lot and it has occurred to me that, had it been something new to Perdita, we would have reacted quite differently. We would have talked about it. We might have gone upstairs to make sure everything was all right.

It has occurred to me that the fact that she tried to hide it from me meant it was something that happened all the time.

And another thing: I don't know who was thumping whom, but whoever was receiving the thumping was used to it too. There was no alarm, no surprise, from the thumpee, just those quiet resigned sort of grunts. It was just another quiet, routine thumping.

This is the thing. This is the thing that keeps me up at night. I thought I was being a good friend for sparing Perdita the embarrassment of having to explain the thumping to me.

I think quite differently now. I think a good friend would ask. I think a good friend *should* ask. Instead of asking, I never went there again.

For this I am entirely to blame.

21

When I woke up I felt guilty, as if we had done something wrong. Far from feeling as if I understood Perdita better, I felt very distant. Her world was so far from anything I had ever experienced.

Harsh as it may seem, I also felt a little bit of contempt for her. She was in denial about what was happening in her life. I thought her denial was cowardly. If she had been as strong as I had previously believed her to be, then she would have been doing something about it. She should be trying to get out.

That morning I had plenty of time to reflect. I felt uneasy about her whole "Let's just pretend this isn't happening" attitude. It wasn't a very adult or practical way to behave. If there was one thing I thought I knew about Perdita, it was that she was adult and practical.

Maybe it was something instinctive in me, something from way back in my evolutionary makeup? Maybe we are wired to keep away from people who are weak or injured? They attract predators. And while we recognize the need for compassion, something deep down makes us wary.

I rang my mother very early in the morning, while Perdita was still sleeping, and asked her to collect me. She was surprised because she usually had to drag me away from a sleepover.

As I packed my bag, Perdita stirred.

"You going?" she mumbled, with an early-morning frown. Her hair was coiled up in long tendrils and stuck to her face.

"Yeah, I've got netball, but thanks," I said, even though I didn't feel the least bit thankful.

All the way home in the car, my mother kept darting sideways looks at me. She asked me if everything was all right and I told her I was just tired.

I was tired, but not sleepy-tired. I was tired of fighting with Candice. I was tired of defending myself against Dara Drinkwater. I was fed up with Perdita's weird, complex life.

When we got home I asked Mum to play a game of Scrabble with me. I thought we could argue about words the way we always had, and then laugh.

Mum agreed but she was distracted. When I tried to

argue with her about words, she didn't argue back or make jokes. She just sighed and picked up her pieces from the board.

"Why won't you play properly?" I asked. My voice sounded like a whine, and I felt cross with myself, and cross with her for making me whine.

"I am playing properly—for first thing in the morning. You do realize what time it is, don't you? It's not even seven o'clock," she replied.

"Yes, but we're not having fun. You're not making me laugh."

"You don't seem to be in a laughing mood."

"This was supposed to *make* me be in a laughing mood," I said.

My mother crossed her arms and leaned back in her chair. "I think you need a nap, grumpy trousers."

I didn't need a nap. I had slept quite soundly. I just wanted to have some normal fun. I just wanted to be in a normal family doing normal, fun family stuff and she was ruining it.

I did something I'd never done before. I picked up the Scrabble board and I threw it across the room. I went to my room to grab my netball gear and I stalked out the front door, slamming it behind me.

I could hear my mother calling from behind me. "What in heaven's name is *wrong* with you, Megan?"

• • •

We won the netball game, but there was a tense moment in the third quarter. Candice was about to do her flying leap thing. She took a run-up and in her last few steps before she took off she said, "Throw it, throw it."

I had the ball. We had never used this maneuver in a Saturday game. It was unpredictable. Nobody knew who was supposed to catch the ball when Candice threw it back into court. It always ended in collisions and spills. That was fine, fun even, when we were playing on the soft surface of the indoor sports center, but this was an asphalt court.

It would be pleasant to say my actions were motivated by concern for my teammates, but the truth was that I was thinking only of that hot-cold burn of grazes on my own legs.

Candice was in the air with her arms stretched out ready to catch the ball. I turned and threw it to Jessica instead. Jessica wasn't expecting it (Candice had called it, and nobody had ever not thrown the ball when Candice called it), but she caught it anyway.

Jessica was off balance and she passed the ball back to Candice, who had just landed. The timing was all wrong. The ball hit her stomach and rebounded to the side. Candice grabbed for it. It was slipping from her fingers and she leaned forward, overbalanced and took two big steps.

When the umpire's whistle blew, Candice looked at me with a face like thunder. I had never seen her look like that before. She looked really ugly. She looked like a spoilt little kid.

I shrugged and smiled. That only made her angrier.

"Don't you *ever* do that again," she said through her teeth.

"Geez, Candice, it's just a game," I said.

"It's *not* just a game, and you know it," she said.

Wow, blow that cool, Candice.

I was pretty angry with her too. It's easy to be uppity about the importance of "the game" when it's no skin off your arse, so to speak.

Candice stormed around the court for the rest of the game with a huge scowl on her face. She made one pass to me with such force that I was nearly winded by it. Afterward she walked off the court without speaking to anyone.

"Hey, Candice," Jessica called after her, "we won, didn't we?"

"What's wrong with her?" Ashley asked.

"I don't know," I replied.

"Don't worry about it, Meggy," said Jessica, patting me on the shoulder. "It wasn't your fault. If it was anyone's fault, it was mine."

"Maybe she's worried about this afternoon?" I suggested. Jessica smiled at me sympathetically. I could tell she was thinking that it was so *caring* of me to think of poor Candice after what had just happened.

The group rallied at Candice's place before the Grand Nudey Run. I went along. I was curious.

Mrs. Perkins was gathering people in groups of three and four to take photos. She radiated cheerfulness.

Candice, on the other hand, was irritable and aggressive. She was getting nervous.

Ashley's mum arrived with the van to pick up the banners and placards. I stood at the back of the group as they lined up to pile into the back.

"Are you coming or what?" snapped Candice, once they were all in.

"There's not enough room. I'll catch up with you down there," I said.

"Are you sure?" asked Jessica. I could tell she was thinking that it was so *self-sacrificing* of me not to go with them.

Candice scowled and slammed the van door.

I ended up going to the Grand Nudey Run with Mrs. Perkins in her Jeep. She was fussing about with a basket of snacks and a cooler full of soft drinks as if we were going on a picnic. As she was driving, she looked out the window at the sky.

"Looks as if it might rain. What a shame. Do you think we should go back and fetch some umbrellas?" she asked.

"It won't matter much, will it?" I replied.

"What do you mean?" she asked.

"Well, they'll be naked," I said.

There was the sort of silence between us that I might have expected if I had just flagged the notion of moving my bowels on Mrs. Perkins's lovely velour car seat covers. I could feel her trying to erase the past few seconds from her mind.

"You do know that they are going to be naked, don't you, Mrs. Perkins?"

"Don't be silly, Megan," said Mrs. Perkins, with a nervous and uncomfortable titter.

I looked out the passenger window and Mrs. Perkins looked straight ahead. I wasn't quite sure what to do. I had a feeling that, being the bearer (pardon the pun) of this particular news, I might somehow be held responsible for it.

"There now," she said. On the side of the road was a huddle of very clothed people. The banner, partly furled, leaned listlessly against the fence. The placards were stacked facedown on the gravel. Candice was standing opposite Michael with her hands over her face.

As Mrs. Perkins parked the car I watched the group. Michael was pointing and gesturing. The group leaned against the police station fence, watching. A cluster of about eight Year 11s and 12s stood nearby, scuffing their feet in the gravel.

"What's happened?" I said as I approached.

"No one will go nude," replied Megan Hadenham.

"It doesn't mean anything," said Candice in a high-pitched voice. "Nothing means anything unless they take their clothes off. This banner, it doesn't mean anything by itself. The police will all look out the window and say, 'Who's Jacob?' Don't you see?"

She turned to Michael. "You *have* to go nude. It was your stupid idea in the first place."

"Me? I'm not going to take my clothes off in public," he replied.

"That was the whole *idea,* you idiot," shrieked Candice.

"I wasn't ever going to do it on my own. I thought the others would. How was I to know they wouldn't do it?"

"You're hopeless! You're such a wuss," shouted Candice.

"Well, how come you've still got your clothes on?" retorted Michael.

Candice glared at him. "Because I'm a *girl,* stupid."

"So?" he shouted back.

Candice turned around and stalked over to her mum's Jeep. She pulled at the handle, but it was locked.

"*Keys,* Mother," she snapped.

Mrs. Perkins pointed the keys at the car and pressed the Unlock button. Candice climbed into the Jeep and slammed the door behind her. She sat in the passenger seat with her arms folded.

One of the Year 12s wandered over to Michael. "Some of the others might do it if it's dark," he suggested. "We could wait until then."

Michael nodded. He looked up at the afternoon sun. "And what should we do between now and then?" he asked.

"Well, we could have a few beers," the Year 12 boy replied. "It might get people in the mood."

A police officer trotted down the steps toward us.

"What's up?" he asked.

The whole group hung their heads sheepishly.

The police officer looked around with his hands on

his hips. The half-folded banner caught his eye. "What's VE JAC?" he asked.

"It's nothing," said Michael.

The police officer cocked his head to the side. "Well, you should probably all go home, then, shouldn't you?"

Michael nodded. The cluster quietly dispersed.

I'd known this campaign would be a disaster. I'd known it the whole time.

22

When I arrived home, Perdita was waiting for me—sitting in the gutter outside my house. I didn't want to see her. It must have shown on my face.

"Prithee, why so pale?" she asked.

"Hay fever," I replied.

Perdita stood up. "There's a secondhand book sale on in the city. There'll be some great stuff there, I'm sure. Last year I found a first edition copy of *The Enormous Room*. I couldn't believe it. It's got to be worth at least a grand, maybe more. There's heaps of crap as well, of course. I'm sure you'll find something."

I tucked my hair behind my ears and looked the other way.

So we're still pretending that last night didn't happen, are we? We're just going to smother it over with a really good book sale.

And why did she always have to make those little cracks at me? She never created a real fight, just those little snide remarks, like pinpricks.

I wondered if she really liked me at all or if I was just the first person who had treated her like a human being. Maybe she was angry with the world, but she knew taking it out on me would ruin our friendship so she just made those little sharp pinprick remarks instead.

"I'm not going."

"It was just a joke. Don't be so sensitive."

"I don't want to go, OK?"

"What else are you going to do?"

I was not in the mood for Perdita's jokes. I started walking up the driveway.

"Where are you going? There'll be a bus in a minute."

"I'm not going," I said without turning around.

"OK," she said, falling into step with me, "we'll stay here, then. What have you got to eat? I'm hungry."

I wondered why Perdita had selected this particular moment to be the most annoying person on the whole planet. Couldn't she see that I wasn't in the mood? She had such poor interpersonal skills. She couldn't read people at all.

My mother was in the kitchen. Her eyes flicked away

from me to Perdita. "Hello there. It's nice to see you again."

"Nice to see you too, Eileen."

I peeked into the living room. The Scrabble board had been put away. I felt a little pang as I imagined my mother there on her hands and knees picking up the Scrabble pieces after my tantrum.

"I'm sorry about before," I mumbled.

My mother nodded. "Never mind. Your father will be home soon. Why don't you two have a swim and I'll barbecue some steaks for lunch."

"Have you got a *pool?*" Perdita asked me. She walked over to the back sliding door and looked out. Her eyes were wide, like a little kid's.

"Yeah."

"Wow, it's got a *waterfall.* You are so lucky," she said. It made me smile. It was a leap from her usual academic manner. I also felt a little bit proud of our pool.

We went to my room, I pulled out an old one-piece for Perdita and she went into the bathroom to change. The phone rang and my mother answered it.

"It's for you," she called out. It was Candice.

"What are you doing?" she asked, gruffly.

"I'm just going for a swim," I said.

"I might come over."

I could tell she wanted to talk. I wasn't sure if she wanted to have a shouting match or a cry.

Perdita came back into my room and sat down on the

141

edge of my bed unself-consciously. She held her clothes in a ball in one hand.

"You'd probably better not," I said into the phone. "We're having a family barbecue."

Candice didn't answer. She had always been invited to family barbecues before.

My mother walked into the room behind me. "Do you want a sausage as well, Perdita?" she asked.

"Yes, please, Eileen."

I closed my eyes and put my hand to my forehead. Candice would have heard that, I was sure of it.

"Maybe another time," Candice said.

Perhaps she didn't hear after all?

"Yeah, sounds good," I said.

Perdita and I jumped in the pool. Mum called out to us from the kitchen window. "I'm just going down the street to get some fresh bread."

We floated on our backs for a while.

"This is so nice," said Perdita. "And you can do this every day if you want."

I showed Perdita how you could stand behind the waterfall. There was a little ledge there to lean on.

"We're *inside* a waterfall," Perdita said, grinning at me. I couldn't help grinning back.

"Do you want to play juss 'tending?"

"What?"

"You know, juss 'tending that we're pirates and we can hide our treasure behind the waterfall."

I laughed. I hadn't played a "juss 'tending" game for about five years.

Perdita's eyes were very bright. There were beads of water caught in her eyelashes. "OK, OK. Juss 'tending that I am the head pirate. I'll be Pirate Don Durk of Dowdee."

"I can't play," I said.

Perdita blinked at me. "What do you mean?"

"I mean that I have lost the capacity to juss 'tend. You show me a stick and tell me it's a sword and I will still see a stick. I just can't do it anymore."

"Of course you can. Everybody can," she said.

I looked at her face and frowned. How could she be so childish?

I heard a voice. "Megan, are you there?"

I frowned again and sat very still.

"Who's that?" whispered Perdita.

I put my finger to my lips, shushing her.

"Megan?" said the voice again.

I stepped through the waterfall. My hair washed down over my eyes. I ducked under the water and ran my hands through my hair, wiping it back out of my face. I resurfaced and opened my eyes. It was Katie Gattrell. She was standing at the edge of the pool with her hands on her hips. What was *she* doing here?

I could see the tie of her bathing suit above her T-shirt. That would be right. The parasite wants to swim in my pool.

"There was no answer at the front door, so I came around the back," she said.

"What do you want?" I asked.

"I was wondering what you were doing. I thought we could just hang out or something."

"I'm busy," I said.

Katie looked around nervously.

"Is there anyone else here?"

"We're having a family barbecue in a little while. Mum's just gone to get some bread before people arrive."

"Oh," said Katie. "Well, what are you doing after that?"

"I don't know how long it will go for. I'll give you a call later if I can, OK?"

"OK," she said. She smiled briefly and then frowned. "See you later, then."

"Yeah, see you," I said.

I trod water, waiting for her to go. Katie stood there at the edge of the pool. She didn't turn around. Why wasn't she leaving?

Just then I heard a splash behind me and Perdita surfaced to my left.

Katie's face went white and she put her hand over her mouth. "Oh my God," she said.

I looked at Perdita and back at Katie. "Oh my God," she said again.

"What are you doing?" I said to Perdita.

"I thought she'd gone," she said, shrugging.

"You should have waited until I told you."

Katie put her hands to her ears. "Oh my *God*. She's wearing your *swimsuit*."

"It's no big deal, Katie," I said.

"No big *deal*?" she said, shaking her head. "The Freak is in your pool, in your *swimsuit*. I can't believe it. This can't be happening."

Perdita ducked under the water and started swimming breaststroke, toward the edge of the pool where Katie stood. She reached the edge, and putting her feet on the floor of the pool, she leapt out of the water and shouted, "Boo!"

Katie screamed and scrambled backward. "Get her away from me! Get her away!"

Perdita stood in the water laughing and pulling faces at Katie. There was a quality to her laughter that put me on edge. It rang in my ears. It was a shrill, hysterical laughter.

"Perdita, stop it!" I shouted. "You're not helping."

Perdita pushed herself off the edge of the pool and floated backward.

"Helping what, Megan? You've been busted. B-U-S-T-E-D. Nothing I can do can make it any worse, so you may as well let me have a little fun."

She moved in toward Katie again.

"Booga, booga, booga," she said in a low growling voice.

Katie took another step back and as her legs hit the outdoor lounge chair, she fell into it.

"Stop it, Perdita. Katie is my *friend,*" I said.

"Not anymore," said Perdita, grinning. She started bouncing around the pool, ducking under the water and leaping out again. Each time she emerged, she let out a whoop. "Whee! Whoa! Woo-hoo!"

I was very angry with her. She was *enjoying* this, but it was more than that. It was weird.

Katie got to her feet and ran down the side of the house. I thought about shouting after her. *It's not what you think. I can explain.* I couldn't explain, though. What sort of excuse could I come up with? How about . . . *Perdita accidentally walked into my backyard and fell into the pool, and we thought we would go for a bit of a swim while her clothes dried.* Or, *I was suffering from some temporary vision impairment and thought she was somebody else.* Maybe *I had hit my head and was concussed and didn't know who I was, let alone who Perdita was?*

No. I could come up with a number of semiplausible reasons why Perdita Wiguiggan should be in my house, but not in my pool, and certainly not in my swimsuit in my pool. There was no excuse. Perdita was clearly here by invitation.

I heard the side gate slam behind Katie.

Now everybody would know about it.

I turned to Perdita, who was still leaping around. "Stop it. Why did you do that?"

She stopped and floated on her back. "What did you expect me to do?"

146

"I don't know, but not jump around like an idiot. If they didn't think you were a freak before, they do now. We could have talked it through, like adults. Now you've ruined everything. Why couldn't you just be normal?"

Perdita stood up. The wickedness in her eyes made me shudder. I don't know what it was about them. They were somehow *wild*. They looked like the eyes of a dog that is biting you in play but any moment now is going to bite you for real. I backed away.

"Well, that's because I'm not normal, Megan," she said quietly. She lifted her arms as if she were swimming butterfly, and lunged toward me. I stepped back.

"Don't do that. You're creeping me out."

"That's because I'm creepy, Megan." She lunged toward me again. "I've always been creepy. You think they call me the Freak because I'm fluffy like a bunny rabbit?"

I was really scared now. Adrenaline streaked through my stomach.

"Get out," I said.

Perdita started to swim breaststroke toward me very slowly. Her eyes were gleaming. "Or what?"

"I said get out!" I shouted, pointing at the gate.

"No way. I'm waiting for my sausage sandwich," she said, smiling. She started to sing a little song.

Waiting for my sandwich,
Waiting for my sandwich,
Waiting for my sandwich.

With each repetition, she moved closer to me. I looked over my shoulder to see how far away I was from the stairs.

I turned and tried to run through the water. It was like a bad dream. I was scrambling and splashing but I couldn't seem to move forward. I could hear Perdita behind me. I could hear her gurgling, squealing laugh and her heavy breath.

I took one last leap and dragged myself toward the stairs. I felt Perdita's hand brush against my heel and I screamed. I dragged myself up the stairs and turned around.

Perdita thrust herself backward and lay in the water, smiling.

"I want you to go home," I said, feeling the water running down my limbs. I was panting.

"Come on, Megan. I was only mucking around. You're too sensitive."

I watched her awkwardly dog-paddling around the pool. From my viewpoint there beside the pool she didn't look very scary at all, but I still wanted her to leave.

I pulled a towel around my waist. I turned around and walked inside, closing the sliding door behind me. I lay on my bed listening to Perdita splashing about in my pool.

After a short time, Mum and Dad came home. Perdita and my parents sat out at the barbecue area, chatting. I could hear the three of them laughing and talking over the sizzle of the barbecue.

Perdita had really frightened me. There was something abnormal about her. But as I listened to her with my mum and dad she sounded perfectly normal.

A little while later my father knocked on my bedroom door. "Are you going to have something to eat, Meggy?"

"No."

"Well, there's plenty if you change your mind."

Then he went away. He didn't try very hard to coax me out of my room. He was supposed to ask me at least twice. Even if he had, I wouldn't have gone. My fear had turned to resentment, particularly when I heard the three of them talking about me.

"I'm awfully sorry, Perdita," said my mother. "It really is terribly childish of her."

"That's no problem, Eileen," replied Perdita lightly.

I wished she would stop calling my mother by her first name. Who did she think she was?

When they finished eating, Perdita and my mother washed the dishes together. I could hear them in the kitchen. Very cozy.

Perdita knocked on the door. "Eileen's taking me home. Do you want to come for a drive?"

"No."

"Can I come in?"

"No."

"Well, I need to get my clothes."

I stood and picked up her clothes, which she had left in a ball next to my bed. I opened the door a crack, pushed the clothes through and closed the door again.

"See you, Megan," Perdita said cheerily, then she was gone.

I lay on my bed with my hands behind my head. I couldn't believe she was leaving without any attempt at an apology.

When my mother came in, I wouldn't look at her.

"We had a nice time with Perdita this afternoon," she said.

"Sounded like it," I said.

"Why didn't you come out?"

"She's *your* little mate, not mine," I said.

My mother smoothed the edge of the doona with her hand. "You know, Megan, I am really beginning to lose patience with your attitude. These last few weeks you have been so bad-tempered. I really don't know what has happened to you," she said.

"Yeah? Why don't you talk to your little mate about it, then?"

My mother sighed and stood up. As she was walking out I called after her. "Well, *Eileen*, I'm beginning to lose patience with you, too. Have you thought about that? No. You're too busy being bosom buddies with your little mate. You know she's really weird. You think she's normal, but she's not. You keep saying there's something wrong with me. Well, why don't you have a closer look at your little mate?"

She turned around. "Your behavior today was embarrassing for your father and me, and it was embarrassing for Perdita. Fortunately, we were able to make the best of it. I think you should stay in here and have a little think about that, don't you?"

Think about it? I had been thinking about it all afternoon. Perdita had ruined my life. She had creeped me out. She had turned my friends against me, and now she had stolen my parents, too.

"Well, I'm *sorry* if you were a little bit embarrassed," I shouted, "but my whole *life* is in the toilet. And you don't even seem to *care*."

"I'm sure you'll get over it," my mother said over her shoulder.

23

REGRET ABOUT THE WOLVES

If only the wolves would howl less loudly
we wouldn't have to explain the way they
sing

if only they wouldn't scare lonely people at
night
we wouldn't have to proclaim how harmless
they are

if only they wouldn't worry children after
school
we wouldn't have to declare them an
endangered species

if only they wouldn't attack and devour our
   domestic pets
we wouldn't have to demonstrate their
   ecological necessity

if only they wouldn't scrape their claws
   against our windows
we wouldn't have to dilate on the loneliness
   of being a wolf

if only they could be persuaded not to collect
   in packs
we could show more easily how each is really
   a loner

if only they weren't so snappish
we could invite them onto our committees

we might even invite them into our homes
if only they acted less hostile

we could even promote a "dialogue with the
   wolves"
if only they showed an interest in
   conversation

we could really prove how we and the wolves
   are one
if only the wolves would agree

if only they'd stop that eternal unnerving
   prowling
we could all sit down at the same table

if only their ears were less sharp
they might hear our side of the argument

if only their eyes were different
perhaps they could see things as we do.

Andrew Taylor

I did not want to go to school on Monday.

There had been complete radio silence on Sunday night. I hadn't heard a peep from anyone.

I didn't even bother getting out of bed. I just lay there watching cartoons.

"You're running late," said my mother, poking her head through the door.

"I'm not going."

"Oh yes you are."

"I'm sick," I said.

"You either get in the shower now, or I'm bringing the hose in," she said. There were two little rosy circles on her cheeks. Her eyes were very bright. She was *really* pissed off.

I got in the shower. I turned up the water so that it was burning hot. I stood under it, feeling the water pummel my back and shoulders. As I got dressed and packed my bag I decided I would go to the bus stop. I would catch the bus and get off at the stop just near the shops.

"See you," I said to my mother as I headed for the door.

"I'm driving you today," she said.

"I'll get the bus."

"You've missed the bus."

"Then I'll catch the late bus."

Mum put her hands on her hips. "I'm driving you to school and I'm going to watch you go inside the gates. I'm going to sit in the car outside the school until I am satisfied that you are going to stay there."

"Haven't you got anything better to do, Eileen? You need a new hobby."

The look on my mother's face was frightening. I'd never seen her like that before. I was scared but I jutted my chin out defiantly.

"Get in the car," she said quietly.

We drove to school in silence. I thought about trying a new tack.

"I really am sick, you know," I said. "You're only going to have to come back and get me later."

My mother didn't look at me. She just kept driving. "I know you're afraid. You're more afraid of someone else than me, otherwise you wouldn't have made such a fuss this morning, but you're going to school today, Megan. You can't hide. You have to go back and face it sooner or later, so it might as well be today."

She pulled up outside the school grounds.

"Off you go, then," she said.

"Can we wait until the bell rings?" I said. "I'll go to class, I swear, but don't make me stand out there in the quad."

Mum pulled on the handbrake. "You know, most of the time, the things you are most frightened about turn out not to be so bad."

"This is very bad," I said, looking out the passenger side window.

"I *guarantee* that you will survive it," she said, patting me on the knee.

"How do you know?" I asked her.

"I went to school too, once, a long time ago. In a couple of years' time you will have trouble even remembering all these people's names, let alone who said what to whom."

I leaned back against the headrest. "You reckon?"

"I reckon."

I looked my mother in the eye. "You know, Perdita really scared me yesterday. There's something about her that frightens me. I don't know what it is."

My mother nodded. "I have felt that too." She sighed and looked out of the front window. "I think she's very intelligent. Having great intelligence but still the emotions of a child can be extremely difficult. I don't know much about her, but she seems to me to be a bit of a lost child. I think she's just trying to cope the only way she knows how, and sometimes she gets it wrong. Maybe you should give her a little leeway?"

The bell rang. I put my hand on the door handle and took a deep breath.

"Give us a kiss," said my mother, leaning toward me.

I kissed her on the cheek. She put her hand on my face.

"I'm proud of you, sweetheart."

• • •

Geography was my first class. When I walked in, Ashley Anderson was sitting with Ryan, one of the boys from Michael Sorrell's group. One look at her anguished and wary face told me she knew. I sat on my own.

I found out that although there have been various evaluations of weed management technologies in the past, most cover only a subset of the relevant issues.

As any fool knows, the benefits of weed management technology depend entirely on the spatial distribution of the weeds.

We discussed (that is, the teacher spoke and we wrote notes on) the factors that influence the level of benefits from weed management and outlined a framework within which the benefits can validly be estimated.

My interest in weed management technology was so piqued by the "discussion" that I felt it necessary to stay back after class (thereby avoiding any need I might have felt to walk with Ashley Anderson) to find out where I might source more information about the different weed management technologies that were available, particularly those in use in rural and regional Australia.

In visual art I learned that during Picasso's "Blue

Period" the adoption of a new tonality indicated a new outlook of melancholic tenderness. On viewing some of these works, we admired the simplicity of their color and the economy of their line, which gave the works an austere nobility. Clearly, this change was due to an adjustment in Picasso's own personal landscape.

We compared this with Jackson Pollock's essentialism, and his pervasive tone of arrested violence. Looking at those pictures, I could clearly see the rage implicit in the works.

Afterward I asked the art teacher if she could perhaps point me in the direction of other painters who have used the color blue.

She was most obliging. We looked at Monet. He used blue quite often, particularly when he was painting water lilies.

I discovered that the color blue was just about everywhere in art, except perhaps in Van Gogh's *Sunflowers*. He painted a whole heap of sunflowers with not a speck of blue to be seen.

I asked the art teacher if she thought this meant that Van Gogh didn't have an outlook of melancholic tenderness. She didn't, but her reasoning took up the whole of recess, which suited me just fine.

After recess I walked into my modern history class and sat down. I saw Candice walk through the door. She didn't sit next to me. She didn't even look at me, choosing a seat on the opposite side of the room. Perhaps other people in the class noticed, but nobody said anything. Nobody ever said anything. We were the group. We were observed and commented upon, but people didn't interfere.

Halfway through the class she called out, "Hey, Megan."

My eyes met hers and I held my breath.

"Do you want to use my green pen?"

We looked at each other across the room. With my expression I thanked her for her discretion. Her eyes were very cold.

I watched with increasing dread as the green pen was passed from one hand to another. I was sure that somebody was going to stop, take out the note and read it aloud to the class.

When it reached me, I removed the stopper and unfurled the note inside. I tried to keep my face as emotionless as possible.

The group wants to talk.
Meet us lunchtime in the room.
You know what it's about.

I had expected something much more spiteful, and for that I was relieved.

At lunchtime I went to the room prepared. After all, I had designed the interventions. I trained the group to use them most effectively. It was simply my turn. On the way to the room I wondered whether the person who designed the lie detector could beat it.

My beanbag had been placed on the opposite side of a semicircle in which my friends were sitting. Candice (the general) was in the middle, flanked by Jessica and Ashley, with Dara, Katie Gattrell and Megan Hadenham on the outside.

The intervention began. Dara Drinkwater contributed nothing, out of what I can only imagine was contempt. Ashley Anderson said nothing because she knew nothing. She had never been particularly good at conflict. Jessica Chou looked genuinely concerned. Megan Hadenham was enjoying being part of the group salvation process. Katie Gattrell was queen. She loved it.

There were no preliminaries; we got straight down to business.

"Megan, you know we really care about you."

"We have talked about it and we don't understand at all."

"We thought it was important that we talk this through together."

"We've had a group meeting."

"You would do the same thing if it were one of us."

"We're really worried about you."

"You're one of the group."

"You're a *founding* member. We don't understand why you would have jeopardized our reputation in this way."

Concern for the group. Nothing personal. They moved quickly and quietly through their lines as if each of us knew they meant nothing. I would have thought that Dara and Katie would relish this, draw it out. Perhaps Candice had muzzled them? I had held them back for her; perhaps she was returning the favor.

"About Perdita."

"You've been hanging out with her."

"How *could* you, Megan? She's a freak."

I folded my arms, realized it was a defensive gesture and unfolded them again.

"So?" I said.

Candice narrowed her eyes and leaned forward.

"The Freak, Megan. You can't possibly be serious. What's *happened* to you? What's *wrong* with you?"

I don't know what's wrong with me. Maybe I've grown. I've outgrown you all. That's what's happened. I don't want to play this game anymore.

I looked at their faces. Nothing I could have said would have made a difference anyway. There was no point defending myself or Perdita.

"What do you want from me?"

Candice sat back in her beanbag. "Are you on some personal crusade, Megan?" she asked. "You and I have been friends for a long time. We've been together through all sorts of things."

Like what, Candice? The occasional grazed knee? You stood on a few prickly weeds and you think we've been through hard times?

"Megan, you invented this process. We need to work this out. We will work it through together. That is what the group is about. That's what makes us strong. You made us this way, Megan. *Together* we sort out our differences."

I looked at Dara. Just for a moment there was a flicker across her face. Was it compassion? From Dara Drinkwater?

"We know that you . . . spent the night at Perdita's house," said Katie. There was a flicker as eyes met eyes. Something was up.

Candice leaned forward. "Megan, are you a lesbian? You know you can tell us."

I laughed. Is *that* what they had been leading up to? Perdita and I must be having a lesbian relationship. That was the only explanation they could come up with.

I had a vision of them sitting around in the coffee shop, all leaning forward with their eyes gleaming. *Megan Tuw's a lesbian.*

"We're just friends," I said.

They all sat back. I think they were disappointed. Megan Hadenham cocked her head to the side as if she didn't believe me. She didn't want to believe me.

"Even so," said Candice, "you see the problem, don't you?"

"Enlighten me, Candice," I said.

"You can't be friends with the Freak and friends with us. You will have to choose."

I sat on my beanbag and thought about it. It was in their power to change the rules. This was the group. They determined what was acceptable and what was not, and they believed Perdita was not. That was the end of the matter.

These people, who claimed to be my friends, could make my life hell, not for a little while, but for years. I knew that because I had taught them how. I had enforced the rules, just as fastidiously and rigidly as they were doing now.

Why did I choose the group? If I am honest with myself, it was laziness. Maintaining integrity is such hard work. The high moral ground must be defended with relentless vigilance and I just didn't have that kind of commitment. Once you are broken, nobody bothers you anymore.

Maybe I just followed the routine? It was habit to spend time with these people. Perdita was hard work. The group was easier.

For whatever reason, I made my decision. If I had my time again perhaps I would do it differently but, as Oprah says, you can only do the best you can with the information you have at the time.

It's done. I can't have my time again. I can't go back.

24

Reentry into the group was not without its price. I had to make a visible commitment. I made it.

Perdita wasn't at school for a couple of days and that bought me some time. I hung out with the group. Dara Drinkwater was allocated the task of supporter, and I bore it. I laughed at Jessica's dumb jokes. I flattered Dara, even though it made me sick. Dara knew it. She extracted those compliments from me like teeth. "What do you think of this color on me, Megan?" "Do you like my shirt?" "Oh, I don't think I'm *that* good-looking, do you think I'm good-looking, Megan?"

I thought that perhaps gorging myself on that humble pie would be enough.

When Perdita did come back to school, she was looking for me. I knew it and I kept away from her. When she was in the corridor I buried myself in the tide moving in the other direction. Each lunchtime I saw her scanning the faces. I turned my face away and blended into the crowd. I tried to flee but she found me.

Perdita walked up to me in the middle of the quad, which was the most conspicuous place. The group was sitting in a circle on the grass. Dara Drinkwater and Katie Gattrell sat on either side of Candice. I sat on the outer edge.

"Megan, I have to talk to you."

I took a deep breath. I could feel the others watching me. I saw Dara and Katie exchange a smile.

"Get away from me."

Confusion crossed Perdita's face and she started to laugh, just a little bit, and then she stopped. She knelt down beside me.

"Megan, I really need to talk to you," she said, quietly and urgently.

I said nothing. I couldn't meet her eyes. I looked at the ground instead, willing her to go. Instead she knelt down in front of me.

"Professor Sabio is not my father," she began.

I tugged at the grass in front of my feet.

Not now, Perdita, not now.

"He called me in to see him. He said he couldn't be, because he is gay. He's never had a relationship with a woman."

165

The group sat silently watching. I could feel them draw back from me, like an audience hushed and expectant before a show.

I looked up quickly. Perdita's lips were drawn down in a grimace. She was holding back emotion, but only just.

"He had the letter. You didn't give him that letter, did you, Megan?"

I looked away. "I didn't, technically."

"Don't you see what this means, Megan? I thought they didn't want me *now*. Do you see? I don't think they wanted me in the first place. They never wanted me."

I pulled at the tufts of grass in front of my crossed feet and stared at the scuffed toes of my shoes.

"Megan?" she whispered. "Why would you do that?"

I raised my eyes to hers and said, "Didn't you hear me? I said get away from me, you freak."

Perdita stammered, "I . . . Megan, please. I need you."

I could see my betrayal reflected back at me and it burned. I turned away.

The group, their smug eyes and cruel mouths drawn into a contemptuous smirk, were savoring the show.

I could tell, because when Perdita walked away, the group called after her, an incoherent rabble-noise at first that became a chorus of jeers. Others joined them in a single chant echoing off the walls of the quad, louder and louder: *"Freak! Freak! Freak!"*

All the time Candice watched my face, daring me to oppose them. I didn't. I watched her lips forming that "F" word, making her pretty face ugly and hard.

It struck me then, looking at her, that I had been deceived all along. Candice was never really my best friend; she just made me feel that way. That was her power. She made everybody feel special, as if they were the most important person in her life. I was no more special to her than Jessica or Dara or Katie Gattrell. She set us up against each other to fight for her attention. She set me up as the bad guy every time, and then who was there to wipe away the tears? Candice, of course.

Why did she pick Dara for the group? She picked Dara Drinkwater as the perfect adversary. I would be so busy fighting Dara that I wouldn't look around me; and I never had.

I'd just betrayed the only real friend I'd ever had, in the most public and unforgivable way.

I wanted to cry but instead I made myself laugh.

I laughed because it was over. I laughed with relief. I had sold my soul to the group and my reward was the understanding of the great charade that it was.

I laughed, painfully, because I knew right at that moment that if I could roll back my life by thirty seconds I would do it differently. You can't roll back your life. Things, once done, are done.

25

When I am dead, my dearest,
Sing no sad songs for me;
Plant thou no roses at my head,
Nor shady cypress tree:
Be the green grass above me
With showers and dewdrops wet;
And if thou wilt, remember,
And if thou wilt, forget.

I shall not see the shadows,
I shall not feel the rain;
I shall not hear the nightingale
Sing on, as if in pain;

And dreaming through the twilight
That doth not rise nor set,
Haply I may remember,
And haply may forget.

Christina Rossetti

Perdita took her own life on a Tuesday.

I didn't find out until Friday. Mr. Tilly told me. He called me out of assembly and into his office. Afterward he called my mother to take me home but I didn't want to go. I went back to class. I sat through a whole day of lessons and said nothing. Nobody else knew.

I played netball on Saturday. We won. It was a perfectly normal game. I went home, opened a packet of chips and lay on my stomach in front of the television.

On Saturday night we were sitting at the dinner table. We were eating chicken. I carefully put down my drumstick and then vomited onto the plate. I sat there looking at it for a moment.

My mother stood up and moved around the table to where I was sitting. She pulled up a chair and put her arms around me. I had started to cry. I didn't even realize I was doing it. I couldn't have stopped if I had tried and I didn't try. My mother didn't try to stop me either. She just sat rocking me in her arms.

I opened my eyes and, over my mother's shoulder, I could see my father cleaning up the plates. He was frowning and tears were rolling down his cheeks. He wiped them away absently with his sleeve. My father was hurting for me.

My throat was sore. I could hear a low hacking, moaning noise. It was me. I was making that noise.

After a while my mother pulled away and my father picked me up in his arms. He carried me to his chair and cradled me, patting me rhythmically on the shoulder. I think I fell asleep, because I can remember waking up. I was still on my father's lap with my head resting against his chin. My mother was sitting on the sofa drinking a cup of coffee.

"You'll have to hop off now, my love. My legs have gone to sleep," he said quietly. I climbed off his lap and moved over to the sofa. I sat next to my mother silently. My cheeks felt hot. I touched them and felt that they were wet. *Is that blood?* I looked at my fingers curiously. Not blood—tears. They dripped from my chin.

I looked at my mother and frowned. "I can't stop crying," I said matter-of-factly.

"I know," she replied.

• • •

On Monday morning at school there was such weeping and gnashing of teeth. Ashley Anderson fainted, and a great deal of fuss was made over her.

All of a sudden it was very fashionable to feel sorry for Perdita, and sorry for ourselves at the loss of her. I think she would have enjoyed it. I didn't know her as well as I would have liked, but I certainly knew her better than these people. I think all these histrionics would have amused her.

I don't remember much about the next few days. I would find myself standing still in the middle of a corridor, like a rock in a river, with students streaming around either side of me.

I felt as if I were in a glass box. I could see people moving around on the other side of it. They were moving in double time. I watched them from inside my glass box.

I had my first panic attack on Wednesday in maths. I think I stopped breathing. When I realized that I had stopped breathing, I suddenly started taking big gasping breaths, but I couldn't feel any air going in.

From my glass box I watched the Denominatrix rushing toward me in that funny little double-time walk that everybody seemed to have taken on. She was shouting at me and shaking my shoulders. I couldn't hear her. All I could hear was organ music, like a merry-go-round inside my head, and a high-pitched buzzing sound.

My mouth opened and closed like a goldfish's. I thought it probably looked pretty funny. It made me laugh out loud thinking about how it looked from outside the glass box. I could feel my muscles contracting with laughter but then I looked down and saw a tiny darkening stain on my shirt, and then another. Tears. I wasn't really laughing at all. I was crying.

How odd, I thought. I looked up at the Denominatrix and the buzzing in my ears got louder and louder and then there were big, white, blurry spots in front of my eyes, and then nothing.

• • •

The next thing I remember, I was in my own bed. I was still in my school uniform, but my shoes were off.

I wondered why I was in bed with my school uniform on. There was something wrong. Something had happened. I lay on my side looking at the posters on my wall. It was like trying to recall a tune when you are listening to another song. It's there, but you can't get a fix on it.

Something bad had happened. What was it?

There was a little chorus running around in my head. A single word repeated over and over, but muffled. I closed my eyes and concentrated. I mentally turned off the other song.

Silence—nothing but birds singing. It was there somewhere. A single syllable, over and over. I could hear my mother moving around in another part of the house. A cupboard door shut. She was in the kitchen. Her feet scuffed across the slate. What was the tune? What was the word? *Here it comes.*

I could hear the clatter of crockery. *Concentrate on the word. Here it comes. It's on the tip of my tongue.*

FREAK! FREAK! FREAK! FREAK! FREAK!

I gasped. It was deafening. I put my hands over my ears, but I couldn't get away. It was inside my head.

"Nnnooooo!" I shouted. The word came from my guts. It tore out of my throat.

I tried to get up, but my legs were tangled in the bed linen. I thrashed to free my legs. I fell to the floor with a crash.

I looked up and my father was in the doorway. His face was white. His mouth was a little "O" of comic surprise. It was Dad in the kitchen, not Mum. They sound the same. I lurched to my feet, still shouting at the top of my lungs, *"No! No! No!"*

My father lunged toward me to help steady me. His face was all concern and tenderness.

"Nnnnooooo!"

I pulled my arm back, and with all the force I could muster, I punched him in the mouth.

26

You could say I took it pretty badly. I didn't
go to school for two weeks. The first week I slept a lot.
The second week there were a few days when I didn't
sleep at all. But I couldn't get out of bed. I just lay there.

My mother brought me food. I remember eating
some toast. My father came into my room too. He sat in
a chair beside my bed. I opened my eyes once and I
could see the big bruise on his face where I had hit him.
I couldn't bear to look at it, so I turned over and faced
the wall until he went away.

Once I heard Candice's voice in the house. My mother
was telling her she couldn't see me.

"Tell her I'm sorry. I'm so sorry," I heard her say.

I sat up in bed and yelled through the doorway, "You should be sorry. Yes, you should be sorry. You *should* be sorry."

My mother came in and put her arms around me, shushing me. "That's not going to help anyone, my darling," she said, rocking me gently.

It was not Candice's fault, though, really. It was my fault. It was my *fault*. I lacked courage. It was me. I did it.

There was a funeral. I went to it dressed neatly in my glass box. The church was full. The group sat in a row in the middle. I stood at the back with my mother and father.

Mr. Tilly gave a very nice speech. Afterward he shook my shoulder briskly.

Mr. and Mrs. Wiguiggan sat together at the front. They looked very tired and old. I had never seen Mr. Wiguiggan before. He was tall and thin with gray hair. His shoulders sloped and his chin jutted out. He looked like Perdita.

After the service my father spoke to Perdita's parents. Mrs. Wiguiggan's face kept crumpling up and distorting.

"He beats her," I said to my mother.

"What?"

"That man. He beats his wife," I said, nodding toward Mr. Wiguiggan.

"Why . . . ," started my mother, and there was a look of

175

understanding between us as we both realized how that sentence was supposed to end: ". . . *didn't you tell me?*"

Good question, Mother. Why didn't I? That's crossed my mind once or twice in the last few days. That's one of the favorite tunes of my midnight "If Only" choir.

Would it have made a difference, do you think? Would it? It was certainly up there in Perdita's "Top 10 Reasons Why I Don't Want to Live," don't you think? Maybe not as high as me calling her a freak in front of six or seven hundred people. Maybe not as high as her recognizing in me, when she was vulnerable and exposed, that I really didn't like her very much, but it's up there.

So, answer me truthfully now, because I have to live with it for the rest of my life, Mother. Would it have made the difference? Would it?

I answered her unasked question. "I don't know."

My mother said nothing. What was there to say? Nothing could be done about it now.

• • •

I wrote Perdita a letter somewhere in that haze.

So maybe you just couldn't cope anymore? You thought you could trust people and it burnt you: first Professor Sabio and then me.

Maybe you saw the true cruelty in the world and decided that you just didn't want to be here anymore.

Was it revenge?

Who's to blame? Me? Or am I the tiger, tiger burning bright—a victim of God's will?

Who, Perdita?

Were you just too lonely, or selfish, or weak? Who's to blame? I don't know.

But I'm *not* sorry. I *refuse* to be sorry. I'm pissed off. You take yourself away from me and leave me with *nothing*. No right of reply. I will have my right of reply. I will have it. Why couldn't you have tried a little bit harder to get through to me?

I refuse to take responsibility. I won't cry. I won't feel sorry. Instead I will learn.

Note to self: bite your tongue. Keep your breath to cool your porridge. Stop it.

I won't cry. Instead, I will live. I will cling tenaciously to my life and I will *never, ever* give up. I'm going to defend the higher ground. And if I fail, I won't kill myself, I'll just stand up and defend it again.

Here's some poetry that you won't recognize:

> You thought I couldn't last without you
> But I'm lastin'
> You thought that I would die without you
> But I'm livin'
> Thought that I would fail without you
> But I'm on top
> Thought it would be over by now
> But it won't stop

Thought that I would self-destruct
But I'm still here
Even in my years to come
I'm still gon' be here

That's Destiny's Child circa 2001, and it speaks as loudly to
me as your Blake or Sylvia Plath or Edgar Allan Poe. It
touches me and it steels my heart.

I have one last thing to say on this subject: I think most
poems are a joke. Don't you get it? All the great poems are
riddled with secret messages that the poets have left in a
language only their nearest and dearest could ever
understand. We try to decode them but I don't think we'll
ever know.
Here's one for you, Perdita.

You were the tiger in lamb's clothing,
You were the thinnest of the thin,
Prizing open my eyes,
To watch them fill with tears,
But I'm a survivor,
And what have you to say to that?
Nothing?
Then I win.

Three months later, at my request,
Professor Emmanuel Sabio led his first community
poetry appreciation class. The classes were held every
second Monday night in the old scout hall (the one behind which the Nudey Boys had hidden).

I had gone to his class the week after Perdita's funeral. He had not been at the funeral because he didn't
know.

Afterward, we sat in the coffee shop. He sat across
from me, rubbing his chin. He didn't say much. He kept
apologizing. "I'm sorry, I'm terribly sorry."

What was he apologizing for? His own behavior?

Now? His treatment of Perdita? My loss, or his own? Maybe all of those things?

I told him about my plan. We would run a class. It would be for everybody. Nobody would feel excluded. We would talk about poetry. People could bring their own if they wanted to.

Professor Sabio wasn't listening. Eventually he stood up and walked away. He didn't say goodbye. It was as if he had forgotten that I was even there. I didn't follow him. I knew what it felt like being inside a glass box.

I stayed in the cafeteria, finished my coffee and paid for them both. On the way out of the university I stopped and put my telephone number in his pigeon-hole with a brief note.

Dear Prof. Sabio,

I'm sorry for your loss.

It would help me very much if we could tell other people about Perdita's passion, which was poetry. Please consider my suggestion and let me know what you think. If you say no I will understand but I will do it anyway. It would probably be much better with your help, because, to be honest, I don't know very much about it.

Megan Tuw

I waited for two weeks, but he didn't phone.

I designed posters and put them up in shop windows and at the supermarket—a little campaign of my own.

Candice came over to my house that week. I stood at

my front door and talked to her through the screen. I told her I wanted to resign from the group. I didn't care what that meant. They could harass me if they wanted to. I didn't care.

Candice stood there, rubbing the sole of her shoe across the doormat. "I would never harass you, Megan," she said. "I don't know if this means anything to you, but there will always be a special place in my heart for you. And if you do want to come back, there will always be a place for you in the group."

Intervention rule number one—hate is not constructive.

I thanked her and then I closed the door. We have not spoken since. I suppose we will talk again at our ten-year high school reunion. We will smile, politely exchange biographies and then move on with our separate lives.

Professor Sabio phoned me a few days before my first poetry night. He said he would like to help.

It ran for four months. It was not very well attended. On a good night we could have up to twenty and on a bad night there were three or four.

It was a mixed bunch. There were elderly ladies who clutched their handbags on their laps, serious young men, precocious wide-eyed children and a few of Professor Sabio's students wearing too much corduroy.

There was a group of three or four Koori ladies, some of whom brought their children. A few of their husbands and friends played touch football on the lawn outside.

My mother and father came to every one. On the third night my father read a poem by E. E. Cummings. He said it was for his lover.

i carry your heart with me(i carry it in
my heart)i am never without it(anywhere
i go you go,my dear;and whatever is done
by only me is your doing,my darling)
                                    i fear
no fate(for you are my fate, my sweet)i want
no world(for beautiful you are my world,my
    true)
and it's you are whatever a moon has always
    meant
and whatever a sun will always sing is you

here is the deepest secret nobody knows
(here is the root of the root and the bud of
    the bud
and the sky of the sky of a tree called
    life;which grows
higher than soul can hope or mind can hide)
and this is the wonder that's keeping the
    stars apart

i carry your heart(i carry it in my heart)

After he'd finished he walked over and he kissed my mother. Everybody cheered and I was proud of them. It occurred to me then that they were really lucky to have found each other.

My mum and dad really were a club of two and I hoped that one day I could find someone who would make me as happy as they made each other.

Things had been a little strained between my father and me after I hit him. He had forgiven me, but I had not forgiven myself.

We talked about poetry in this little group. Sometimes we made up plays, too. On colder days we made tea in Styrofoam cups, swapping the cups from hand to hand to keep warm.

There was a boy who joined the poetry group just before the end. His name was Simon. He was a big fan of T. S. Eliot. A couple of times we sat outside beneath green orange boughs after the group had gone and talked about tomorrow.

After much coaxing, he told me his last name. It was Goose. He blushed when he told me and mumbled something about having a bit of a rough time at school.

Simon Goose was a nice boy and I liked him very much. I would not let him down, not for anybody. He was my second chance. Life is full of second chances, if you stick around.

By the spring the class had petered out. I was sad that it ended but it didn't matter. I didn't have bad dreams anymore.

Guilt was the most difficult thing for me. Not guilt

for what I had done as much as guilt for not *liking* Perdita very much. I often wonder if we could have got past that, and I suspect that we could have, given time.

I would have felt better about it if we had parted on good terms, if I had had the chance to get to know her better. But then, if we had been on good terms, it wouldn't have ended, et cetera, et cetera.

By spring my guilt had been replaced by thoughts of the High School Certificate and a kind of restrained exhilaration about my future.

I sat with Angela and her friends at school. They weren't like the group, but there was a quiet, respectful kind of camaraderie that suited me.

I watched the group from the outside. Like everyone else in our year, I was aware of their dramas, romances and victories. Their actions were studied and discussed like the royal family's. For the first time I was glad I was no longer on display.

On the last night of the community poetry appreciation class, Professor Sabio and I were alone.

We sat together on the grass at the front of the scout hall, leaning back on our arms. He told me a story about a young woman he once knew called Perdita Wiguiggan, who had stolen half an arts degree and then robbed herself of a rich life.

He told me that one day Perdita had come to his office and asked whether he might be her father, and he had told her that he was not.

"What I didn't tell her, and it may be the one thing I

will regret in my life, was that, of all the students I have ever taught, Perdita was not the best, but the one who I enjoyed teaching the most. I will not have children. It makes me sad. But if I did, I hope they would be individual, and true to themselves—as she was. I wish that when Perdita came to me that day, I had told her that although she was not my daughter, I would have been proud if she had been."

Perdita was the most uncompromising person I have ever met, and when I think of her now, that is the quality I admire the most. It's also the quality that made her choose to die. I think she gave up on the world, and gave up on me, too soon. The thing that most disappoints me is that Perdita was not around to see that I too have learned the enterprise in walking naked.

author's note

This is a novel about many things, including school politics, personal responsibility and how different people react when they are thrown together. It also touches on the issue of suicide. I recognize that Perdita's death may touch a raw nerve for a few readers. There are agencies that can help if you need counseling for yourself, or if you want advice on what to do about someone you know who is contemplating suicide:

National Hopeline Network
Twenty-four hours a day, seven days a week
1-800-SUICIDE

about the author

ALYSSA BRUGMAN attended five different schools in New South Wales, Australia, and completed a business degree at Newcastle University. She began writing at age twenty-two. She now lives in Sydney and is a full-time writer. *Walking Naked* is her U.S. debut.

Alyssa Brugman's Web site is www.geocities.com/alyssabrugman.

A READERS GUIDE

walking naked

alyssa brugman

"A painful look at the naked truth."
—*Kirkus Reviews*

1. Take another look at the Yeats poem at the beginning of chapter two. What is your interpretation of the poem? Have you ever had your "song" taken from you?

2. Megan says that she and her friends use the "interventions" to "identify and remove elements that might cause conflict between us. . . . It was a very adult way to resolve disputes" (p. 37). Do you think Megan is accurate in describing the purpose of the interventions? In what other ways could such conflict be handled? Why is it considered conflict in the first place?

3. On page 49, Megan tries to spin the group's rejection of Katie with positive words. When does this same technique get turned on Megan herself? How do you think it affects her?

4. *"I've always prided myself on my frankness and honesty"* (p. 82). Do you think Megan is an honest person? How does she change in this respect from the beginning to the end of the book?

5. *"I know I wouldn't have stepped outside my front door in the jeans she was wearing. Why was that?"* (p. 99). Perdita makes Megan question her beliefs about the social order of high school. Who decides what you have to do to be cool or popular? What are some reasons you have for trying to fit that model, or for rejecting it?

6. Why do you think the author chose to start a chapter with the poem "Regret About the Wolves" (p. 152) at this point in the book? Who is the wolf? What does the poem say about the way we treat social outcasts?

7. On page 167, Megan seems to realize for the first time what her friendship with Candice is really about. Have you ever had an eye-opening moment when your perspective on someone you thought you knew was totally changed, for good or bad?

8. What do you think Megan thinks of Perdita toward the end of the book? Does Megan want to be friends with her? Have you ever known anyone who strongly influenced you or changed your life without your really liking them or being friends with them?

9. Look back at the last couple of chapters in the book. What does Megan feel after Perdita's suicide? How did you react when you read that Perdita had killed herself?

10. *"Perdita was the most uncompromising person I have ever met"* (p. 185). What does Megan mean by "uncompromising"? Have you ever compromised yourself or your beliefs for the sake of social convention or popularity? Have you ever refused to do so?

In her own words—

a conversation with
Alyssa Brugman

Q. How did these characters and this story evolve in your mind? What drew you to the subject of popularity?

A. One of the things about school is that you are thrown together in a year level with about a hundred people who are the same age as you, and who live in roughly the same area, but these are really the only two things you have in common. This doesn't happen at any other stage in your life.

I decided to see what would happen when I put two young people in the same room who were ideologically opposed. It was important that I removed Megan from her friends, because within that circle she is invincible. They needed to meet as closely as possible to equals, and Perdita was already at a disadvantage, so I made her more capable academically to make up for the mismatch in social skills. Once I put them in that space the story pretty much wrote itself.

Q. Did you draw from any of your own specific experiences or observations in high school? Did you ever have a rough time of it? Do you identify at all with Megan or Perdita?

A. In everything that I write there are things that did happen, and things that didn't happen, and things that happened but in a different way.

I once caught an airport transfer bus from Melbourne airport to a writers' festival in Bendigo, which is about two hours' drive. The other people on the bus were very tired, and a bit smelly, and it was clearly the final leg of a long overseas trip for them. The whole trip was silent, and after about an hour and a half I had a sudden urge to sing "Ninety-nine Bottles of Beer on the Wall." I didn't.

Real life tends just to be a sequence of events, but when you depict them in fiction then the events have to have meaning and a purpose. If I were to put that scene in a novel then I would make it a normal public bus rather than an airport transfer bus, because the dynamic is more flexible. I would have a character for irritation—say a baby that won't stop crying—and for comic relief—someone listening to a personal CD player and singing loudly and off-key, but not being aware of it. I would include a long description of a character on the bus whom we have not met yet, but who will be important to the story later on. I would not make the destination Bendigo, because I am not familiar enough with the city to portray it in a story. And my main character would definitely sing "Ninety-nine Bottles of Beer on the Wall."

When you get to the end of the story it is true that there are parts within it that have happened to me, but I bend, expand, and contract to give it meaning and purpose, so that even those things that are real are impossible to extract from those that are fiction. I am neither Megan nor Perdita—I am both. I am also Megan's father and mother, and Gordon Gordon Library Warden, Ashley Anderson, and Simon Goose, because they all live inside my brain constructed from a mishmash of memories and fabrications to suit the needs of story.

Q. Why did you want to include poetry in the book, and how did you select the particular poems?

6

A. I included the poems for three reasons:

1. When I was at school and we studied poetry it was all about Grecian urns and conscientious objection, and very dead people. It had nothing to do with my life, and I was not moved by a single poem. It was not until a long time after I left school that I discovered poetry, and it started with W. H. Auden, T. S. Eliot, Ezra Pound, and then others later. I started reading voraciously and began to see what I had read everywhere—in movies, on TV, in books, in other poems (writers sending cryptic messages to each other and paying their respects). I learned the secret delight in allusions. I wanted my readers to discover that pleasure earlier than I did, so I tried to find a range of poetry from different centuries in different styles that reflected what was happening in the girls' lives. I spent a long time searching for exactly the right poems, and it was exhilarating when I found them. I had not read the work of Andrew Taylor and Pattiann Rogers until I began researching material for this book, so they are two new favorites.

2. When I began to write dialogue for Perdita she was very circumlocutory, and I had a great deal of trouble getting her to spill, and Megan wasn't going to ask, but I knew the reader needed to know, so I had to find a vehicle whereby she could tell us what was happening for her. The poetry was an apt device for her character.

3. I thought English teachers would dig it and buy class sets, and I could give up my day job. They did and I have.

Q. Have you ever tried your hand at writing poetry? How do you think the process compares to writing a novel?

A. I like to try lots of different writing styles—poems, plays, short stories, horror, sci-fi, you name it. I think experimenting with other forms and styles and learning how they work will help develop both my core strength and my range. I don't know that the process is so different. I write everything quickly and from my gut, and then I whittle away at it afterward.

Q. Life is very difficult for Perdita, yet we never directly see what's going through her head. Did you ever consider writing the book from her perspective?

A. Frankly, I wasn't very interested in Perdita's perspective. Given her background and her character, her behavior is easy to justify. Megan, on the other hand, has wealth, stability, beauty, intelligence, strong interpersonal skills, and high self-esteem—in other words, no excuse whatsoever to be so brutal. The challenge was to not only justify her actions so that the reader believes them, but to bring the readership around to a point where they actually cry for Megan.

I wrote it from Megan's perspective, and it is through her eyes that we see, but the dialogue and actions of all the other characters have to be real. So, for example, Megan describes how her mother sits, stands, speaks, and what she says, but I have to think about what her mother's true response to the situation would be, given her background and attributes, in order to make Megan's description accurate to the reader. So when I am writing a character—any character—I have to write that bit from their perspective, even though we may hear it from someone else.

Q. **Megan talks a lot about being frank and honest. What are some of the more honest, tell-it-like-it-is books or authors that you have read that inspired you?**

A. Australia produces a lot of great YA books. Some Aussie authors that stand out for me are Sonya Hartnett, Phillip Gwynne, Ian Bone, and also Bernard Beckett (he's from New Zealand). From the States I liked Robert Cormier and Paul Zindel when I was growing up, but I'm not familiar with any of your current YA authors.

Q. **Do you like writing for young adults? Do you write for adults and younger children as well?**

A. I tried writing a picture book once, and I thought it was good but my publisher said it sucked, so I went back to the YA stuff. Not all of the time, but most of the time when I sit down in front of a blank screen, the voice that begins to speak is somewhere in the range between twelve and nineteen. I don't know why that is.

When you write about an adult, then you need to give them an occupation, because it takes up a large proportion of their time. In order to make that vocation sound credible you need to do research. Even with secondary adult characters, such as Megan's parents in this book, it was necessary for me to do a little bit of research about their jobs. I prefer to spend my time exploring the relationships between characters, rather than dedicating slabs of time researching things that are external to the characters. It would be tempting, when writing an adult, to use one of my own previous jobs, because I could write about it with authenticity without researching, but if I were to do that then everyone would assume that the character is me, no matter how strenuously I refuted it. Teenagers are easier to write about in that way because everyone has been to school and people of all ages, and in most cultures, recognize that environment. I can focus my attention on the dynamic and conflict between the characters, which is where the joy in writing is for me.

Q. Do you think about your characters after you finish writing the book? Do you ever imagine what they would be up to now?

A. No. I am writing a series at the moment and so I need to insert possibilities in the early books that will leave space for my protagonist to grow in later books, but that is a technical device, rather than any emotional attachment to her. I normally work on a number of projects at once; so while one draft is with my editor I write the next draft of the next project. When they are finished and out there on the shelves I don't really think about them at all. I am much more haunted by characters who have not yet had their stories told!

Stargirl
JERRY SPINELLI · 0-440-41677-9
Stargirl. From the day she arrives at quiet Mica High in a burst of color and sound, the hallways hum with the murmur of "Stargirl, Stargirl." The students are enchanted. Then they turn on her.

Ghost Boy
IAIN LAWRENCE · 0-440-41668-X
Fourteen-year-old Harold Kline is an albino—an outcast. When the circus comes to town, Harold runs off to join it in hopes of discovering who he is and what he wants in life. Is he a circus freak or just a normal guy?

Borrowed Light
ANNA FIENBERG · 0-440-22876-X
Sixteen-year-old Callisto May feels a deep connection to astronomy. She can name all the moons of Jupiter and even tell you the dimensions of the Great Red Spot. But she feels completely alone on planet Earth. And now that she's pregnant, her loneliness is acute.

Crooked
TOM AND LAURA MCNEAL · 0-440-22946-4
Clara and Amos search for honesty and meaning in the ninth grade—where thrills, heartbreak, and intimidation can take place at a locker, in the lunchroom, or in a bathroom stall.

Counting Stars
DAVID ALMOND · 0-440-41826-7

With stories that shimmer and vibrate in the bright heat of memory, David Almond creates a glowing mosaic of his life growing up in a large, loving Catholic family in north-eastern England.

Heaven Eyes
DAVID ALMOND · 0-440-22910-3

Erin Law and her friends in the orphanage are labeled Damaged Children. They run away one night, traveling downriver on a raft. What they find on their journey is stranger than you can imagine.

Before We Were Free
JULIA ALVAREZ · 0-440-23784-X

Under a dictatorship in the Dominican Republic in 1960, young Anita lives through a fight for freedom that changes her world forever.

Becoming Mary Mehan: Two Novels
JENNIFER ARMSTRONG 0-440-22961-8

Set against the events of the American Civil War, *The Dreams of Mairhe Mehan* depicts an Irish immigrant girl and her family, struggling to find their place in the war-torn country. *Mary Mehan Awake* takes up Mary's story after the war, when she must begin a journey of renewal.

The Sisterhood of the Traveling Pants
ANN BRASHARES · 0-385-73058-6

Over a few bags of cheese puffs, four girls decide to form a sisterhood and take the vow of the Sisterhood of the Traveling Pants. The next morning, they say goodbye. And then the journey of the Pants, and the most memorable summer of their lives, begin.

A Great and Terrible Beauty
LIBBA BRAY · 0-385-73231-7

Sixteen-year-old Gemma Doyle is sent to the Spence Academy in London after tragedy strikes her family in India. Lonely, guilt-ridden, and prone to visions of the future that have an uncomfortable habit of coming true, Gemma finds her reception a chilly one. But at Spence, Gemma's power to attract the supernatural unfolds; she becomes entangled with the school's most powerful girls and discovers her mother's connection to a shadowy group called the Order. A curl-up-under-the-covers Victorian gothic.

Colibrí
ANN CAMERON · 0-440-42052-0

At age four, Colibrí was kidnapped from her parents in Guatemala City, and ever since then she's traveled with Uncle, who believes Colibrí will lead him to treasure. Danger mounts as Uncle grows desperate for his fortune—and as Colibrí grows daring in seeking her freedom.

The Chocolate War
ROBERT CORMIER · 0-375-82987-3

Jerry Renault dares to disturb the universe in this groundbreaking and now classic novel, an unflinching portrait of corruption and cruelty in a boys' prep school.

Dr. Franklin's Island
ANN HALAM • 0-440-23781-5

A plane crash leaves Semi, Miranda, and Arnie stranded on a tropical island, totally alone. Or so they think. Dr. Franklin is a mad scientist who has set up his laboratory on the island, and the three teens are perfect subjects for his frightening experiments in genetic engineering.

Keeper of the Night
KIMBERLY WILLIS HOLT • 0-553-49441-4

Living on the island of Guam, a place lush with memories and tradition, young Isabel struggles to protect her family and cope with growing up after her mother's suicide.

When Zachary Beaver Came to Town
KIMBERLY WILLIS HOLT • 0-440-23841-2

Toby's small, sleepy Texas town is about to get a jolt with the arrival of Zachary Beaver, billed as the fattest boy in the world. Toby is in for a summer unlike any other—a summer sure to change his life.

The Parallel Universe of Liars
KATHLEEN JEFFRIE JOHNSON • 0-440-23852-8

Surrounded by superficiality, infidelity, and lies, Robin, a self-described chunk, isn't sure what to make of her hunky neighbor's sexual advances, or of the attention paid her by a new boy in town who seems to notice more than her body.

The Lightkeeper's Daughter
IAIN LAWRENCE • 0-385-73127-2

Imagine growing up on a tiny island with no one but your family. For Squid McCrae, returning to the island after three years away unleashes a storm of bittersweet memories, revelations, and accusations surrounding her brother's death.

Girl, 15, Charming but Insane
SUE LIMB • 0-385-73215-5

With her hilariously active imagination, Jess Jordan has a tendency to complicate her life, but now, as she's finally getting closer to her crush, she's determined to keep things under control. Readers will fall in love with Sue Limb's insanely optimistic heroine.

The Silent Boy
LOIS LOWRY • 0-440-41980-8

When tragedy strikes a small turn-of-the-century town, only Katy realizes what the gentle, silent boy did for his family. He meant to help, not harm. It didn't turn out that way.

Shades of Simon Gray
JOYCE MCDONALD • 0-440-22804-2

Simon is the ideal teenager—smart, reliable, hardworking, trustworthy. Or is he? After Simon's car crashes into a tree and he slips into a coma, another portrait of him begins to emerge.

Zipped
LAURA AND TOM MCNEAL • 0-375-83098-7

In a suspenseful novel of betrayal, forgiveness, and first love, fifteen-year-old Mick Nichols opens an e-mail he was never meant to see—and learns a terrible secret.

Harmony
RITA MURPHY • 0-440-22923-5

Power is coursing through Harmony—the power to affect the universe with her energy. This is a frightening gift for a girl who has always hated being different, and Harmony must decide whether to hide her abilities or embrace the consequences—good and bad—of her full strength.

Cuba 15
NANCY OSA • 0-385-73233-3
Violet Paz's upcoming *quinceañero*, a girl's traditional fifteenth-birthday coming-of-age ceremony, awakens her interest in her Cuban roots—and sparks a fire of conflicting feelings about Cuba within her family.

Both Sides Now
RUTH PENNEBAKER • 0-440-22933-2
A compelling look at breast cancer through the eyes of a mother and daughter. Liza must learn a few life lessons from her mother, Rebecca, about the power of family.

Her Father's Daughter
MOLLIE POUPENEY • 0-440-22879-4
As she matures from a feisty tomboy of seven to a spirited young woman of fourteen, Maggie discovers that the only constant in her life of endless new homes and new faces is her ever-emerging sense of herself.

Pool Boy
MICHAEL SIMMONS • 0-385-73196-5
Brett Gerson is the kind of guy you love to hate—until his father is thrown in prison and Brett has to give up the good life. That's when some swimming pools enter his world and change everything.

Milkweed
JERRY SPINELLI • 0-440-42005-9
He's a boy called Jew. Gypsy. Stopthief. Runt. He's a boy who lives in the streets of Warsaw. He's a boy who wants to be a Nazi someday, with tall, shiny jackboots of his own. Until the day that suddenly makes him change his mind—the day he realizes it's safest of all to be nobody.